THE MOB

Written by

G. R. Holton
And
Marlene Mendoza

World Castle Publishing

G. R. Holton & Marlene Mendoza

This is a work of fiction. Names, characters, places, and incidents are products of the author's imagination or are used fictitiously and are not to be construed as real. Any resemblance to actual events, locations, organizations, or person, living or dead, is entirely coincidental.

WCP

World Castle Publishing
Pensacola, Florida

Copyright © G. R. Holton and Marlene Mendoza 2013
ISBN: 9781939865441
First Edition World Castle Publishing June 15, 2013
http://www.worldcastlepublishing.com

Cover: Karen Fuller
Editor: Maxine Bringenberg

G. R. Holton & Marlene Mendoza

Dedication

In honor of our mothers
Donna Holton
And
Margaret Pacholka

G. R. Holton & Marlene Mendoza

Chapter One
Daddy's Little Girl

It was November 10, 1914, in the big city of Chicago. The area was somewhat quiet other than the stories that were being told about the mob; stories about insurance payments, territory disputes, numbers running, gambling, and sometimes even murder.

A happily married couple named Anthony and Brigitta Cachiotti sat on the stairway to their apartment, enjoying the beautifully warm fall evening. They were very much in love. Anthony was a tall, thin man with dark wavy hair, while Brigitta was petite, with long flowing black hair and dark brown eyes. She was slightly overweight from eating her momma's Italian cooking, but Anthony still loved her with all of his heart.

Tonight was a special night for the Cachiotti's, and Brigitta was about to make Anthony the happiest man on Earth.

"Anthony, I went to see my doctor this afternoon."

"You didn't tell me you had an appointment. Is everything all right?"

"Everything is great. But I do have something that I really need to talk to you about."

"What is it, dear?" Anthony asked with deep concern in his voice. "You sure nothing is wrong?"

"Nothing is wrong, but you are going to be a daddy!" Brigitta told him, with a smile beaming on her face.

"Really? Are you sure?"

"Yes, my love, I am very sure. I was well over a month late, so my mother and I went to see Doctor Jenkins. He ran some tests, and I am about two months pregnant."

Anthony wrapped Brigitta in his arms. "That's absolutely wonderful. I can't believe it…I am going to be a daddy! I love you so much."

"I love you too. We will have to fix up that spare bedroom for a nursery now instead of a storage room."

"Oh, that will be great. I will turn it into the best little nursery ever!"

Anthony and Brigitta kissed and held each other tightly.

***

On June 5, 1915, Brigitta was in the hospital delivery room, having just given birth to her first child…a little girl. The doctor placed the baby on Brigitta's chest.

"You have a beautiful baby girl, Mrs. Cachiotti. Shall we bring in your husband?" asked the head nurse.

"Oh, she is beautiful. Yes, please ask Anthony to come in."

The nurse walked out of the room and went to the waiting room.

"Mr. Cachiotti, would you please follow me?"

"Is everything okay?"

"Everything is just fine. You are the father of a very beautiful baby girl."

"I was hoping for a girl! That is great news!"

Anthony and the head nurse went into the delivery room, and he went straight to Brigitta and the baby. He gazed upon the baby with tears flowing down his cheeks.

"Oh, Brigitta, you did so great! She is absolutely beautiful. What should we name her?"

"I think we should name her Maria Louisa after her two grandmothers."

"That is a perfect name, Brigitta. I couldn't have thought of two more beautiful names."

"Well, you helped, my husband. Look...she has your eyes."

"She is going to grow up to look like her momma though. Can I hold her?"

"Sure, honey. Be gentle though. She is a fragile little thing."

"I will be."

Brigitta lifted up the little girl and Anthony took her into his arms.

"Oh, Maria...you are the most beautiful thing I have ever seen. I promise you I will take care of you till the day I die."

Anthony stood there rocking Maria back and forth.

"Okay, Mr. Cachiotti, let's give the baby back to her momma, and you need to leave for now. You can come back in about an hour. We need to show momma a couple of things."

"Oh, do I really have to?"

"Yes, Mr. Cachiotti, but as I said, you can come back soon."

Anthony handed the baby back to Brigitta, and then bent over and gave her a kiss on her forehead.

"I love you so much. I will be back shortly."

"I love you too."

***

Time passed quickly, and Maria was getting bigger by the day.

On a sunny spring afternoon four years later, Maria and her father were in the park. Maria asked questions while her father pushed her on the swing.

"Daddy, why Momma's belly getting so big?"

"Sweetie, that is because your momma is going to have a baby. You are going to have a sister or a brother."

"I gonna have a siser?"

"Well, it may be a brother. We won't know until Momma has the baby."

"But I no wanna baby."

"We don't have a choice, Maria. You will be a big sister, and you need to love the baby."

"I no wanna baby, and I no will love it!"

"Maria, no matter what, I am always going to be your daddy, and you will always be Daddy's little girl."

"I love you, Daddy."

"I love you too, kiddo."

***

Six months had passed, and Maria and Anthony were in the hospital waiting room while Brigitta was in the delivery room. Several hours went by before the nurse came into the waiting area.

"Mr. Cachiotti, your wife has had some complications during delivery."

"What happened? Is she okay? What about the baby…is it okay?"

"Mrs. Cachiotti is going to be okay. The baby was born with the cord around her neck, and it caused distress to the mother. You have a baby daughter and she is doing well. But Mrs. Cachiotti lost a considerable amount of blood and needs to rest."

"But they're both going to be okay?"

"Yes, Mr. Cachiotti. Both are resting, but they need to sleep for a while."

"So I can't see them?"

"No, I am sorry, not tonight. You can come back tomorrow morning to see them. I assure you they are fine."

"As long as you are sure they are okay. Maria, we need to get our coats on."

"I want to see Momma!"

"You can see her tomorrow. Tonight we will stay at your nana's house, okay?"

"Daddy, I want Momma."

"You can see her tomorrow. Now let's go."

Maria put on her coat and they walked out of the hospital.

"Daddy, is my mommy going to live?"

"Yes, Maria. The doctors and nurses will take very good care of her."

"Okay, as long as you said so."

Anthony and Maria walked down the street to Brigitta's mother's house.

***

The following morning Maria and Anthony were in the room with Brigitta.

"The baby is so little. Daddy, was I that little?"

"Yes, you were."

"I am big now."

"Yes, and you are the big sister, so you will have to help your mommy, okay?"

"I will do that, Daddy."

"Now my wife, what are we going to name this bundle of joy?"

"Well, since I feel that she is a blessing, I want to name her Theresa, but I am not sure of a middle name."

"Let me think for a second. I know…how about Carolina?"

"Theresa Carolina Cachiotti; that is just perfect, Anthony."

"Maria, meet your baby sister Theresa."

"Hi, 'Resa. My name Maria, and I is you big siser. Can I please hold her, Momma?"

"Sure, go sit in the chair and Daddy will bring her over."

Anthony picked up Theresa from Brigitta's arms and placed her on Maria's lap.

"Okay, baby 'Resa. You have to listen to me. I am the big siser."

"So, Maria. Do you love your baby sister now?"

"I will love her as long as she don't touch my toys."

***

As the months passed, Maria and her father spent a lot of time together. Although he tried not to show favoritism, Maria was the apple of his eye. He would take her and her sister to the park, to the country to fly kites, and find everything imaginable for a daughter and her dad to do. Every night, before Maria went to bed, her father would sit and say prayers with her, and then sing her a lullaby so she would go to sleep.

Months turned into years, and Maria always clung to her father's side.

G. R. Holton & Marlene Mendoza

Chapter Two
The Loss of Daddy

In June of 1925, Anthony and Brigitta's little Maria was turning ten years old. Every day she would hang out the window to watch for her father to return home from work.

It was a typical summer day for everyone else. The neighborhood children played cops and robbers or skipped ropes in the street. But for Maria, the day was special, as it was her tenth birthday. On the sidewalk was a stand that was filled with all types of fruits and vegetables. A kind, elderly, Italian man named Salvatori Pegrini stood with his sleeves rolled up, peddling his wares, as Brigitta walked up to his stand.

"Well, good'a morning, Miss Cachiotti. How are you this'a beautiful day?"

"I am doing great, Mr. Pegrini. I pray all is well with you."

"I'm'a doing fine. What can I get'ta for you today?"

"I need three large tomatoes. Today is Maria's birthday, and she loves Pasta e Fagioli, so I am going to make a nice dinner and a cake for her."

"Oh, that sounds'a wonderful. I love Fagioli," Mr. Pegrini said as he reached over and placed three of his best tomatoes in a paper bag. "That's'a nice. How old is she?"

"She turns ten today. They get so big so fast."

"I know…all'a my little ones are having little ones. Here'a you go. That'a will be'a two cents please."

Brigitta reached into her purse, removed the two pennies, and handed them to Mr. Pegrini.

"Food is getting so expensive, but we must eat."

"I know…everything is'a getting so expensive. It'sa hard to make a living any more. I tell'a you what. Take this and'a give it to Maria. Tell'a her I said 'Buon Compleanno.'" Mr. Pegrini grabbed an apple and handed it to Brigitta.

"Grazie, Mr. Pegrini. I know she will love it."

Brigitta placed the apple in the bag with the tomatoes.

"You have a great day, Mr. Pegrini."

"You too, Mrs. Cachiotti."

Brigitta walked away from the stand, down the street, and then up the stairway to her apartment.

***

Just blocks away from the Cachiotti home was the hardware store in which Anthony worked. The Colombo Hardware store was one of the oldest businesses in the area. Guiseppi Colombo was the owner of the store, and he got it from his father, who got it from his father. Now Guiseppi was sixty-five years old and thin as a rail, but there was not a harder worker in all of South Chicago. Guiseppi was almost like a father to Anthony, because his had been killed during the Spanish-American War, and Mr. Colombo would have done anything for him.

Late in the day, Anthony was trying to finish stocking the shelves towards the back of the store. As he lifted another box to go on the shelf, he heard the bell ring in the front of the store, which signified that a customer had walked in. Anthony quickly placed the box on the floor and went to the front to take care of who ever had come in.

When he got to the front counter he saw two young men dressed in suits and wearing fedoras; Antonio Capresi and Jack Palmero, gangsters who worked for Pasqaule Bianchi, the godfather over all of South Chicago. Antonio was a handsome man who had run numbers for Mr. Bianchi since he was fourteen. Jack Palermo was a little older than Antonio, and obviously had quite a problem with acne that had left him scarred.

"Well, well, well, Mr. Colombo. I hope that business has been good this week," Antonio said.

"Now'a you listen here, I don'ta want no trouble," Mr. Colombo replied.

"There isn't going to be any trouble. Mr. Bianchi just wants his money." Jack leaned on the counter and placed a toothpick in his mouth.

"I don'ta care about what'a your boss wants. You tell'a your boss I no pay. He has'a no right to take'a my money. I'm a poor man just trying to make a living."

17

"The boss is really not happy hearing that from you all the time, and you know what happens to people that don't pay their insurance." Antonio made his way to the end of the counter.

Anthony made his way over and stood beside Mr. Colombo, making sure he was between him and Antonio.

"It is really simple, Mr. Colombo. All you have to do is give us the money and we will leave you alone," Jack continued.

"I'a told you. I have'a no money for your insurance. Now the two of you grease'a balls need to get out'ta of my store and never come back. Anthony, throw out this scum."

"Okay, you two. You heard Mr. Colombo. Get out and don't bother coming back."

"Anthony, you're making a big mistake. Maybe you should reconsider what you're saying," Antonio replied with a snarl.

"I don't give a shit. You two are nothing but puppets for Bianchi. So unless you're deaf, you heard Mr. Colombo. Now you two just turn around and get the hell out of here!"

The two men went to walk out the door, but Jack Palermo turned back to face Anthony. He pointed at him and cocked his thumb as if he was firing a pistol.

"We will be back. You can take that to the bank."

"You will get the same answer. Now leave."

Antonio and Jack walked out the door and Anthony turned to face Mr. Colombo.

"Don't worry about those guys. They are big on talk, but they are just cowards."

"I'a know, Anthony, but they cause'a me so much'a trouble all the time. I'a know one of these'a days they may just'a do something."

"I am here, so don't you worry."

"You don'ta know how much'a I appreciate you being here to watch over me."

"Mr. Colombo, you are like my father in so many ways. I feel that it is an honor to work for you."

"I'a knew your father. He was a great'a man. If it wasn't for my bad'a back, I would have'a joined him in that'a battle he died in. So, I'm a lucky man in some'a ways."

"Well, hopefully we took care of those guys for awhile."

"They'a will be back some'atime, and my answer will'a always be the same."

"You just need to be safe going home, Mr. Colombo. I don't need you getting off'd on your way home."

"Oh, Anthony, you just'a worry about yourself. I will'a be fine. They won't get any money if'a they kill me."

"I should get back to work. I have half a pallet left to shelf and I will be done."

***

After Antonio and Jack walked out of the store, they got into a large, black, 1925 Studebaker.

"Antonio, you know that sooner or later Mr. Bianchi isn't going to put up with this shit from Colombo."

"Yeah, I know. What I don't like is that Anthony character. I think he needs to take a trip in a Chicago overcoat."

"You're right. Let's hit him tonight after he leaves work. Maybe then Mr. Colombo will be a little freer with the loot."

They pulled down the street and parked, waiting for Anthony to leave the store for the evening.

***

Anthony was in the front of the store, making sure the counter was wiped down, when Mr. Colombo came out from the back of the store.

"Mr. Colombo, I have everything cleaned and put up. Would you mind if I left a bit early today? I wouldn't ask, but it is my little Maria's tenth birthday, and I want to get home to celebrate."

"Oh, that is'a nice. Sure, you go right ahead."

"Thanks so much."

Anthony took off his smock and hung it on a hook on the wall.

"Okay, Mr. Colombo, I will see you in the morning."

"Please be'a careful going home. I trust'a Bianchi and his bunch as far as I can'a throw them. And for a man'a my age, that is not'a very far."

"I will, Mr. Colombo."

Anthony stepped out the door and closed it behind him, then headed down the sidewalk toward his apartment. He didn't notice the car that followed him as he walked along.

As he turned the corner, he saw Maria with her head out the window.

"Papa! Papa!"

"Hey, how is my little birthday girl?"

As Anthony began to walk up the stairs, the Studebaker pulled up to the curb, screeching its tires. Two men, Capresi and Palmero, got out and opened fire with machine guns.

"That will teach you, Mr. Anthony. Maybe now your boss will listen," Antonio yelled out, laughing.

The bullets ripped through Anthony, and he fell to the stairs, bleeding profusely.

***

Maria watched intently as both Capresi and Palermo jumped back into the car and it sped off down the street. She pulled her head in from the window and screamed at the top of her lungs.

"Papa! Papa! Momma, they shot Papa!"

Brigitta pulled Maria away from the window.

"Maria, you need to take your sister to your room."

Brigitta ran out the kitchen door to the hallway with Maria close behind her. They hurried down the stairs and through the doorway, and went quickly to Anthony's side. Brigitta cried as she held Anthony to her bosom. His breath was labored as he slowly closed his eyes and died. At the same time, Maria wiped the tears that ran down her face.

"Papa...I saw him. I saw his face. I will never forget that smile and his laugh. I will find out who he is! I promise I will make him pay someday! I promise."

***

Outside a nightclub on Chicago's lower southeast side, a neon sign spelled out "Eldorado Club" to pierce the darkness. Antonio pulled up to the curb and turned off the engine. He stepped out of the vehicle and walked over to a young man who stood in front of the door to the club.

"Hey there, David, keep an eye on my baby. Make sure that no one scratches her."

"Sure thing, Mr. Capresi."

Antonio walked through the doorway, and was immediately engulfed in the cloud of smoke created by all the cigar smokers in the lounge. In a corner booth sat a group of well-dressed gentlemen with a few scantily dressed females. He made his way over to their table, where he found Demetrio DeSilva, Jackie Marchetti, and Joey Petriani.

"Good evening, Mr. DeSilva."

"Well, Antonio, it's good to see you. I assume that you know Jackie and Joey."

"Yes I do. How ya doing, fellas?"

"Hey, Antonio," Jackie stated.

"Ant...how ya doing?" asked Joey.

"I am just aces, Joey; and you?"

"You know...just swell."

"So, Antonio, are you just out having a good time, or did you need to speak with me?" asked Demetrio.

"Actually, Mr. DeSilva, I do need to speak with you about something very important, and not for other ears."

"Okay, ladies, why don't you go powder your noses or something?"

The three women got up from their seats and walked away.

"Antonio, have a seat. Would you like some vino?"

"Sure, thanks; that would be great."

Antonio pulled out a seat next to Mr. DeSilva and sat down.

"What do you have on your mind?" Mr. DeSilva asked as he proceeded to pour Antonio a glass of wine.

"Mr. DeSilva, I think that I have taken care of the problem from Giuseppe's store. He shouldn't be a problem for you anymore."

"Why do you say that?"

"Let's just say that one of Mr. Colombo's workers just got a bad case of lead poisoning."

"I pray it was a clean hit."

"Yes, sir. No one saw us."

"You say us. Who was with you?"

"Oh, I'm sorry. It was me and Jack Palermo."

"Very good. So, do you think Mr. Colombo will pay his insurance now?"

"I think our point was made. I will be visiting him in a few days to collect."

"If you keep this up, Antonio, you will definitely go places within the family. Mr. Bianchi awards for good service, and I will make sure he is aware of your contributions."

"Grazie, Mr. DeSilva. I really appreciate that."

Chapter Three
Maria Begins Her Mission

The months passed slowly for Brigitta and the girls, and as time went by, months turned into years. Five years passed, and Maria Cachiotti had become quite the teenager. Now fifteen years old, she loved to sing, but not only because she loved music. She was already plotting to make the gangster that had killed her father pay for what he had done. Her mother had moved the girls to a different apartment building in a quieter area of South Chicago, but she was still close to the Eldorado Club, to which she had followed Antonio many times since she had been given permission to walk by herself. She began to spend her weekends across from the club to watch Antonio come and go. She would also hang out at the back of the club and listen to the jazz singing from inside. As she stood there, she learned all the songs.

***

One afternoon Maria stood at the back door of the club and waited for the young lady that had been singing to exit. The woman was a young, voluptuous blonde by the name of Susan Rey.

"Excuse me, ma'am, my name is Maria Cachiotti. I have been listening to you sing, and you sound like an angel," Maria said as she walked alongside Susan.

"Well thank you, young lady."

"I listen to you every day that I can, and I was wondering if you would be willing to teach me how to sing like you."

"That all depends on a few things. The first one is your parents; will they let you get lessons from a lounge singer?"

"Well, I just have my mom. My father was killed when I was young, but I think she would be okay with it."

"The second thing is that I can't do it for free. I hope you understand, but I have to pay bills."

"How much would you charge? My mom only works as a waitress and does some sewing on the side, so we don't have a lot of money to spare."

"I'll tell you what. I will give you singing lessons for a dime an hour, and maybe your mom could do some sewing for me to cover the rest of it."

"Thank you so much. I will ask her tonight and let you know if that is all right."

"That would be fine, Maria. My name is Susan."

"It is very nice to finally talk to you, Susan. I need to run home or I will be late for supper."

"You better run on then, young lady. We don't want you to be late."

"See ya," Maria yelled as she turned and ran off.

The Mob

***

Later that evening Brigitta, Maria, and her sister Theresa all sat in the kitchen eating their supper.

"Momma, how would you feel about me taking singing lessons?"

"Well, Maria, that would be nice, but I am not sure we can afford it right now."

"But, Momma, I have met someone that would only charge a dime for an hour of lessons, and maybe some sewing for her costumes."

"Where did you meet this person?"

"She is the singer at the Eldorado Club. She is really good, and I know that she can teach me. It is what I have dreamed of doing, Momma."

"What? The Eldorado Club? Young lady, what have I told you about hanging out there? Nothing but sinners and gangsters hang out there."

"But Momma, I really want to sing, and I love listening to her from outside the back door."

"I really don't like this idea, Maria, but I know how you love singing. I would want to meet her before I agree. I think if she will take most of her payments in sewing then we can do it. Have her come over this Saturday for lunch and we will talk."

Maria jumped up from her chair, ran over, and hugged her mother with tears running down her face.

"You are the best, Momma!"

"Okay, go sit back down and finish your meal."

Maria went back to her chair and literally hopped into it. She finished her supper, went to her room, and started to sing.

***

The following afternoon after school, Maria stood at the back door of the club until Miss Rey stepped outside for her break.

"Well, hello, Maria. How are you doing today?"

"I am doing great, Miss Rey. I talked to my mother, and she would like to meet you. She said to invite you to Saturday lunch at our house."

"First off, you can call me Susan. Secondly, I would love to have lunch with you, but I have to be at the club at 2 p.m. to sing."

"Okay, Miss Susan. I will tell Mom that you will come. We live at 723 East Avenue, Apartment 34. We always have lunch at noon, and you will love my momma's cooking."

"It will be great to have a home-cooked meal that I don't have to cook. I will see you then."

"Fantastic! I will tell my momma that you will come. I need to run off now to go get my homework done."

"Okay; have a great night and I will see you on Saturday."

Maria headed for home as Susan went back inside the club to finish her set.

***

Saturday had come, and what Maria felt was more than just excitement. She paced back and forth in the living room as time ticked away. She hoped her mother liked Susan as much as she did, and that they would be able to afford the lessons. No one else realized that this was all part of Maria's plan to exact revenge on

Antonio. She lived every day thinking how he would be paid back for what he had done.

The clock read noon straight up when a knock sounded on the apartment door.

"I will get it!" Maria yelled, already running toward the door. "Who is it?"

"It is Susan Rey from the Eldorado."

Maria opened the door and greeted the tall, blonde singer.

"Good afternoon, Miss Susan."

"Well, good afternoon to you too."

"Momma, it is Miss Susan," Maria called out toward the kitchen.

"I'll be right out. Take her jacket and hang it up."

"Okay, Momma. May I take your jacket, Miss Susan?"

"Thanks."

Susan removed her jacket and Maria hung it up on the coat hanger that was beside the door.

"We can go into the living room. It will be more comfortable there. Can I get you a glass of lemonade, or would you prefer coffee?"

"Coffee would be great. You will learn that lemonade isn't a good choice just before singing."

"I will try to remember that."

Just then Brigitta came out of the kitchen.

"Well, hello, you must be Susan. I am Brigitta, Maria's mom."

"It is very nice to meet you, Brigitta. You have quite the daughter here."

"Thanks; she can be a handful. But she is also my little angel. Things have been hard on her since we lost her father, so when she said she wanted to sing, I thought it would be a great distraction for her."

"Momma, I offered Miss Susan a drink. Would you like some coffee too?"

"That would be nice, Maria. Just be careful in the kitchen, okay?"

"Oh Momma, you know that I will."

Maria got up from the couch and went into the kitchen.

"So, Susan, tell me a little about you."

"Well, I am originally from Louisiana. I lost my parents in a house fire at a very young age. I just happened to be at my grandparents' house that night, and so they raised me. I took an interest in singing at the age of eight, and have been doing it ever since. I hope someday to make it to Broadway, or maybe even have a show in Las Vegas at one of those big, fancy hotels."

"I am so sorry to hear about your parents. How long have you been living in Chicago?"

"Oh I guess about five years now. I had a friend who was supposed to get me into the theater here, but that fell through, and I had no choice but to take the job at the Eldorado."

Maria came out from the kitchen and placed the coffee on the coffee table.

"Here you go, Miss Susan. I didn't know if you wanted cream or sugar, so I brought them out anyway."

"Thanks so much. I don't use milk, for the same reason I don't drink lemonade."

"I will try to remember that too, Miss Susan."

"Susan, Maria says that you would be willing to give her singing lessons for a dime an hour, plus some sewing."

"Yeah...I hate to have to charge anything, but I have to pay bills. Really, the sewing is what would help the most. I need some better costumes for singing, but can't afford a seamstress."

"I fully understand. I work as a waitress down the street and barely make ends meet. If you would let me do the sewing for you and maybe charge a nickel an hour, then I can swing that. I really want Maria to be able to follow her dream."

"I know it must be hard being a mother of two and trying to pay the bills. Maria reminds me of myself when I was her age. I'll tell you what I will do. How about seven cents an hour and the sewing? I will even take her into the club when it is closed once in a while so we can use the piano. That way I can teach her what I know about playing it, also."

Suddenly a timer buzzed in the kitchen.

"Oh there's lunch. I hope you like lasagna."

"I love it. In fact, I haven't had any in a long time."

"Well, let me get it out and we will finish talking," Brigitta said as she got up from her chair. "Maria and Theresa, I need you girls to set the table."

Theresa ran in from the kitchen.

"Okay, Momma," Maria answered.

"Susan, why don't you go ahead and make yourself comfortable? Lunch will be ready in just a couple of minutes."

"Is there anything I can help you with?"

"Oh no, that's okay. You just relax. You are our guest," Brigitta replied as she walked into the kitchen.

Within minutes the four of them were sitting at the dining table and talking as they ate their meal.

"I have to say, Brigitta, this is one of the best lasagnas I have ever had."

"Oh thanks; it is a recipe that my grandmother handed down from old Italy. She was one of the best cooks, and she taught everyone how to cook also. You know what? I have an idea; how about you come here on Saturday afternoons to give Maria her lesson? I will make lunch and work on your outfits, and you charge the nickel. You get sewing and a nice home-cooked meal, and Maria gets her lessons."

"You have got yourself a deal. I don't get many home-cooked meals, so it will be well worth it."

***

As the weeks went by, Susan and Maria got together to sing and Brigitta always cooked great lunches. Susan brought fabric and all the sewing supplies, as well as drawings that she had done of dress ideas. Brigitta sewed as the two girls sang, and while her voice could not begin to measure up to Maria's, sometimes Theresa joined in the singing. Susan quickly began to feel like part of the family.

***

The Mob

One afternoon, the two singers were together at the Eldorado Club, and the old Negro piano player, a man who went by the name "Smokey," walked in as they were in the middle of a song. They immediately stopped singing, as Smokey had startled them.

"Well, hello, ladies. May I ask what you two are doing here so early?"

"Hey, Smokey. Yeah, I am giving a singing lesson to young Maria here."

"Hi, Maria, it is a pleasure to meet you. They call me Smokey. Has Susan taught you anything yet?"

"Yes, Mr. Smokey. She is a great teacher. She even taught me a little bit on your piano."

"So, Miss Susan is touching my piano, huh? Naughty girl. I'm just kidding. So, Maria, what is your favorite song?"

"Well, Mr. Smokey, I have tried a bunch, but I think my favorite right now is 'What Is This Thing Called Love?'"

"First off, you can just call me Smokey. I know that song; it is a great little number. Do you want me to play it so you can practice it?"

"Would you, Smokey?" Maria replied.

"I wouldn't have asked if I wasn't planning on it. Miss Susan needs to practice it anyway," Smokey said, laughing.

"Well then Smokey, let's get to it," Susan said.

Smokey played the song for each of the girls. After each one had sung, Smokey stopped and gave them some helpful instructions.

***

A year of singing classes and piano lessons had gone by, and Maria was now quite the singer. She practiced all the time. She often stood in front of the Eldorado Club, and as the songs played inside, she sang along with them until she perfected her renditions. She learned every jazz song there was as she watched for Antonio to arrive. She learned the names of everyone in the Bianchi family as they came and went. But every time she saw Antonio her anger level grew, and she knew that no matter what it took he had to pay for what he had done to her father.

***

One Saturday afternoon Susan arrived at the apartment at her usual time. They had lunch and Maria helped clear the table as she always did before her lesson. Once finished, she went into the living room with Susan.

"Maria, we need to talk."

"What's wrong, Miss Susan?"

"Oh dear, there is nothing wrong. But I think I have taught you everything I can about singing. You have turned into quite the little songbird. At your age I couldn't sing any better than you do right now. I want you to keep practicing, though, and maybe your mom can get a radio with the money she has been spending on your lessons. That way you can start learning all the current songs to practice."

"Are you sure, Miss Susan? I bet there are still things I can learn from you." Maria was on the verge of tears.

"Believe me, I will miss your momma's cooking, but it is time for you to move on. Please don't cry."

"I will just miss you is all. But I will keep practicing like you said, and someday I will be a famous singer too."

Just then Brigitta walked into the room.

"Maria, why are you crying?"

"Well, Momma, Miss Susan says today is the last lesson."

"Yes, Brigitta, I have taught her all I can. Maybe you can get her a radio and she can practice with it?"

"I will miss your company at lunch. If you're ever in need of any sewing, please feel free to let me know."

"To be totally honest with you, Brigitta, I will be moving. I've got a job in New York City singing with the Dorsey Brothers' band."

"That is fantastic! Congratulations...I wish you all the best."

"Thanks a bunch."

"So that means I will never see you again?" Maria cried even harder as she ran over and hugged Susan.

"I am sorry, Maria, but yeah, I have to go. It is my big chance. When you get older you will understand."

"Maria, someday, when you get older, you will probably move away too. Maybe you will go to New York and be a famous singer like Susan."

"I know, Momma; I am just going to miss her. Miss Susan, I understand, and I will pray for you that it is the answer to your dreams."

"I will miss you too, kiddo. But you keep practicing, and maybe someday we will sing together on stage."

"I would like that."

"Well, I need to go home and get packing. Thanks so much, Brigitta, for all the sewing you have done, and for the great meals. I'm surprised my new clothes fit!"

"You are quite welcome."

Brigitta opened the door and Susan went to leave, but Maria ran to her again and hugged her tightly.

"I am going to miss you!"

"I will miss you too."

Maria let go of her and Susan headed down the stairs. Maria ran to the window and watched as Susan walked down the street.

"Momma, someday I am going to be a great singer just like Miss Susan."

"Oh, Maria…somehow, deep in my heart, I know that you're will leave here someday and do just that."

Chapter Four
Let the Games Begin

As each year passed, Maria became more and more beautiful. She was a stunning young woman with long black hair that flowed down to the center of her back. Her singing voice was top notch, and she knew just about every jazz song that was ever written.

It was now 1935 and Maria had just turned twenty years old. She knew that it was time to set her plan into motion, so she dolled herself up and headed to the Eldorado Club.

A sign in the window read, "Singer Needed—Apply Inside." Once she stepped inside she was hit with an overpowering stench of old cigar smoke. Smokey sat at his piano, and an old drunk was slumped over the end of the bar.

The owner, Rico Cianci, was behind the bar cleaning glasses. Rico was a short, dark haired, heavy-set man with an olive complexion. He was known around town as quite the womanizer, and he treated his singers as if they were his personal slaves. But Maria

G. R. Holton & Marlene Mendoza

knew that if she was going to get close to Antonio, she had no choice but to sing in Cianci's club.

"Good afternoon, Mr. Cianci."

"Well, well; what brings a babe like you into my humble abode?"

"I see you have an opening for a singer."

"You're a looker and a singer too?"

"Yes, I have been singing all my life. You've got to give me a chance. I promise you won't be disappointed. Just ask Smokey over there. He was around back when Susan was training me."

"So, Susan Rey trained you and you know Smokey…now that is very interesting. Okay, go get up on stage. But if you want to be a singer in my joint, you better be a canary."

Maria made her way through the tables and stepped onto the stage. Smokey was playing a jazz tune and seemed to be in his old little world, so Maria walked over to him, placed her hand on his shoulder, and bent over to speak in his ear.

"Hey there, Smokey. Can you play 'Ain't Misbehavin' for me?"

"I can play anything you want, Miss Maria."

Maria walked to the microphone as Smokey began to play the song. When she started to sing, Mr. Cianci stopped what he was doing and seemed transfixed by her voice. As soon as she finished she walked off the stage and to the bar where Cianci stood.

"Wow, babe, where did you get pipes like that?"

"I listened to a lot of records, took those singing lessons, and hung around outside here. I know you have more going on in this place than just your typical lounge, but don't worry, Mr. Cianci...mum's the word."

"It better be, babe, 'cause if not, someone will ensure you never sing again. Be here tonight at five, and make sure you wear something really sexy."

"Oh, don't you worry. I'll be here."

Maria walked over to the window, took down the "Singer Needed" sign, and tossed it onto the bar.

"You won't need this any longer."

Maria walked out the front door and headed straight home. She was excited to tell her mother what she had accomplished.

"Momma!" Maria yelled as she came through the door.

"Hey, Maria. So how did it go?"

"Well, I got the job."

"You know I don't like this one bit. You could be playing with fire."

"I know what I am doing. Antonio is going to pay...but first I have to get as much trash on him as I can."

"I still don't like it. On top of everything, you're working in that dive! The only people that go in there are the scum of the earth. Nothing but lowlifes and gangsters, I tell you."

"Momma, I know, and I know you are worried. But I have to do this for Papa."

"I know you do. Please be safe, okay?"

"I will. Now, I need to look sexy tonight. Maybe that hot red number I got?"

"Oh Mary, Mother of God, please protect her," Brigitta prayed, kissing her rosary beads.

Maria walked into her bedroom and closed the door, but it opened again immediately when her kid sister Theresa walked in.

"Hey, sis, I heard you telling Momma that you got the gig at the Eldorado."

"Yeah, Theresa, I got it. Now I can start setting the bait to get Antonio."

"I agree with Momma. You are going to get yourself in hot water!"

"Listen, you both just need to trust me on this. I know what I am doing. I have followed that piece of trash all over town, and this is where he hangs out and picks up women. I just have to get him to pick me up, and treat him so special that he won't be able to live without me."

"So you are really going to marry the shithead that murdered our father?"

"That is the plan...and you need to watch your mouth. You're talking about my future husband." Maria started to laugh.

Theresa laughed with her. "You are so bad. But if you ever need my help you know that I am here for you. I can be quite sneaky myself."

"You never know, I might have to take you up on that someday."

Maria started to go through her dresses that hung in the closet.

"Okay, what outfit do you think?" Maria asked, eying each one critically.

"If you're going for sexy, then it has to be the red one. It will make his eyeballs fall out."

"You're right, the red one it is. I am going to take a nice hot bath to relax and then get dressed. I will be honest with you, sis. I am a bit nervous about getting up there and singing."

"Maria, you sing better than most of them women on the radio. You will knock them dead."

"I guess you're right. Can you tell Mom that I won't eat until I get home tonight? My stomach has butterflies right now."

***

A couple of hours later Maria was in her dressing room in the back of the club, putting on her makeup, when there was a knock on the door.

"Hey, canary, you go on in ten minutes. I sure hope you are ready for this," yelled Rico Cianci.

"Yeah, I'm ready Rico. Could you put some water on the stage for me, please?"

"Sure, babe. I will give you whatever you need, and even more if you let me."

"In your dreams, Rico," Maria laughed. "Just the water, okay?"

"Yeah…whatever. Ten minutes!"

Maria finished putting on her makeup and got up from her vanity. She stepped back, checked her appearance in the mirror, and looked toward the ceiling. "Okay, Papa…this is for you. Please be with me on this. It is the only way I know of to avenge your death."

Maria walked out the door and headed to the stage, where she found Smokey already at the piano.

"Smokey, are you ready for this?"

"I am always ready, Miss Maria; you should know that by now," Smokey laughed.

"Alrighty then, let's do this."

Maria walked up to the microphone and Smokey began to play "Ain't Misbehavin'."

Maria sang while customers filled the lounge.

***

After a few hours Antonio finally came into the club and went to the corner table where Demetrio DeSilva sat.

"Do you mind if I join you, Mr. DeSilva?"

"Sure, have a seat Antonio. I am just checking out the new canary on stage."

Antonio sat down and faced the stage.

"So, Antonio, how are things going in the neighborhood?"

"Things are going well, Mr. DeSilva. Actually, I think I can handle a lot more than what I am doing now. But I know Mr. Bianchi sees that I am doing a good job. Someday I think he will make me an underboss."

"Don't you be getting too cocky! You're a good man and he knows that. Just don't get too big for your britches. I know you're keen to everything, and you have a lot of potential. In time, you will become a key player, but for now just keep doing your job."

"I plan on it, Mr. DeSilva."

"Don't worry…I tell Mr. Bianchi everything, and he is very pleased with your work."

"Thank you, Mr. DeSilva, that sure does mean a lot to me. So, what do you think of the new dame up on stage? She is, how you say, 'provocante'!"

"She is definitely a sweet patootie. Why don't you check her out?"

Antonio laughed. "I assure you, at this moment I am. A dame with gams like that needs a good man like me to sink his meat hooks into her."

"You have a good night, Antonio. It is getting late and I need to be going home." Demetrio stood up and put on his jacket. "Don't do anything I wouldn't do."

"Oh, I will be sure of that. You have a good night, Mr. DeSilva."

Demetrio walked out the door as Antonio continued to watch Maria.

***

As she finished her last song and walked off the stage, headed toward the bar, Antonio got up from his seat and met her halfway.

"Hey there, doll. My name is Antonio, and I would be honored if you would join me at my table for a drink."

"I only have fifteen minutes, and I have to go in back and change for the second set. Maybe we can get some coffee later on. I get off at one...that is, if you want to stick around."

"If you're going to be singing till then, I will definitely be here."

"Well then, coffee after closing. I need to go back to my dressing room and change."

"I will be here."

Antonio went back to his table as Maria walked to her dressing room to change.

"Okay, I have just set the bait. Now I have to take my time luring him in, and he will be right where I want him," Maria said to herself as she changed her dress.

***

At one o'clock in the morning Maria finished for the night. She seductively walked down from the stage, smiling over at where Antonio was seated.

"Antonio, I need to go change. Can you meet me around back in, say, ten minutes?"

"Sure babe. Not a problem. I will pull the car around back."

A few minutes later, Maria stepped out the back door and found Antonio waiting in his black Studebaker. Maria knew that car very well...it was the same car that he had driven when he killed her father.

Antonio got out and came around to open the door for Maria. Once she got inside, Antonio closed the door, then went back around the front and got inside. He drove just a few blocks and pulled over in front of Babe's Diner. Babe's was a small diner, but at that time of night it did a steady business from drunks who were looking for a hot meal before heading home.

Antonio got out of the car and quickly came around and opened the door for Maria. The two of them walked up to the diner and stepped inside. There were a few people inside, so Maria and Antonio went to the far corner and sat in a booth.

"What can I get you guys?" asked the waitress.

"I will have some coffee," Antonio answered. "What about you, Maria?"

"I think I will just have some tea. I need to be able to sleep tonight."

The waitress walked away and Antonio pulled out a cigar.

"I hope you don't mind. I like a cigar with my coffee."

"No, I don't mind at all. In fact, I love the smell of a good cigar," Maria lied; she actually hated the smell.

Antonio lit his cigar and blew a ring of smoke into the air.

"You know something, you can really sing. How long have you been at it?"

"Oh, I started singing when I was about ten. I have always loved music, and my father would sing to me when he put me to bed."

"Well, I have never heard anyone with pipes like yours. You sing beautifully."

"Thanks so much. So, speaking of jobs, what do you do for work?"

"I guess you could say I work in insurance and taxes."

"Oh, so you're a government man."

"No, I actually work for a private firm."

"Oh, okay. So are you originally from here?"

"Yeah, I was born here. But my family originally came from Sicily. In fact, most of my family still lives out there. My parents were here for a few years, but moved back after I turned eighteen. How about you? You live in Chi-town all your life?"

"No. Actually, we lived in East Moline. We moved here when I was about five-years-old, when my father was looking for work."

"What kind of work does he do?"

"Oh, he left us when I was young. We never saw him again. My mom raised both me and my baby sister."

"I am sorry to hear about your father."

Sure you are, you son of a bitch.

"Thanks, but I know someday I will see him again…probably when I die and go to Heaven."

"Anyway, let's change the subject. How would you like to join me for dinner sometime next week?"

"I think that would be really nice. I am actually off on Thursday, if that is okay for you."

"Thursday would be just great. That actually works out well for my schedule too. How about I pick you up around seven o'clock then?"

"That is fine. Here is my address."

Maria took a pencil out and wrote her address on a napkin, then handed it to Antonio.

***

An hour passed as they talked, and at three o'clock Maria decided to call it a night.

"Antonio, if you don't mind, it is getting late, and I have to get up early."

"Yeah you're right, it is getting pretty late. How about you let me give you a ride home?"

"No, that's okay, I will be fine. I'm just a couple of blocks from here. The walk will actually help me get to sleep."

"That's your choice, kiddo. I will see you at the club then."

"I wouldn't miss it for the world." Maria smiled, but all the while her hatred for him burned inside her like a furnace.

The two stood up and Antonio helped Maria put on her jacket. Maria left the diner as Antonio grabbed his jacket, threw a dollar bill on the table, and followed her out the door.

G. R. Holton & Marlene Mendoza

Chapter Five
Dating Your Death

On Thursday morning Antonio got up and made his usual rounds, but all the while couldn't keep his mind off Maria.

That night Antonio was at Maria's apartment at precisely seven o'clock. When Maria opened the door, Antonio's mouth dropped open when he saw her in a long, black, low cut dress that was slit up the side. He cleared his throat, and pulled a dozen long stemmed roses from behind his back.

"Beautiful flowers for a very beautiful woman. I have to say it though; you are just togged to the bricks."

"Why thank you, Antonio. At least I am not being called a doll or a dame. I hate those labels."

"Yeah, I guess men use those names a bit too much. I sure hope you like Italian food."

"You're talking to a good old-fashioned Italian girl. I love food that is cooked well. But it has to be good...nothing like what Guy's Place tries to pass off as authentic."

"That is great, because I am taking you to a little place outside of Chicago. It is a ways out there, but I assure you that the food will be more than worth the ride."

"That is fine by me. Why don't you come in for a moment while I put these flowers in water and get my jacket?"

"Thanks, don't mind if I do. You have anything to wet the ole whistle before we head out?"

"Yeah, I have some very old Scotch that my father never finished. It is on the counter there by the couch. Let me get you a glass."

"That would be great."

Antonio stepped into the apartment and Maria took the flowers into the kitchen. She then returned shortly with the glass. Antonio was already in the living room, so she walked over and handed it to him.

"I hope you like it. It was one of his favorites. I will be right back…I need to get my stuff and we can head out."

"Sure, Maria, not a problem," Antonio answered as he poured a glass of the Scotch.

Maria returned moments later with her jacket and purse. Antonio helped her put the jacket on.

"Well, thanks so much, Antonio. You are quite the gentleman."

"I do know how to treat a lady, my dear. You ready to go?"

"Let's hit the road. Just set the glass on the table. I will get it later."

Maria opened the door and Antonio walked out. Maria turned around and locked the door, then followed Antonio down the stairway to the front door, which Antonio opened to allow Maria to precede him. Antonio hurried to the car and opened Maria's door for her, and she climbed into the long black car that she remembered all too well. The memory overwhelmed her for a moment, and a tear ran down her cheek.

"Are you okay, Maria?"

"Oh yeah, I am fine. I just got a piece of dust in my eye. You know these roads are so dusty sometime."

Maria removed a tissue from her handbag and wiped the tear away.

"I just wanted to make sure you're okay."

Antonio climbed into the driver's seat and started the engine.

"Okay, let's ride," he said with a smile.

***

After two hours of driving, Antonio pulled up in front of a small restaurant. A sign above the doorway read "Little Giovanni's."

"Here we are, Maria. I sure hope you like it. It is one of my favorite out of the way places to eat."

"I am sure that if you like it, then I will also."

Antonio walked around to open the car door for Maria.

"You know, Mr. Capresi, a girl could get use to this special treatment." Maria smiled at him.

"I don't do it for everyone, only someone as beautiful as you."

"That's so sweet."

Antonio took Maria by the hand and led her into the small Italian restaurant, where three of the five tables were unoccupied, and one of them in the far back corner had a "Reserved" sign on it. A stout, short, gray-haired man came out from the kitchen, his apron covered with spaghetti sauce and other unidentifiable items. He walked over and hugged Antonio, kissing him on each cheek.

"Antonio, it is'a so nice'a to see you again. I have'a your table ready."

"Giovanni, this is the girl I was telling you about. Maria, this is Giovanni. He is a longtime family friend."

"Oh, Antonio, she is'a as beautiful as you said'a she was."

"It is nice to meet you, Giovanni. You have a lovely little place here."

"Thank you. Please'a, have a seat, and I will get you a nice bottle of Barsac. It is a very nice'a wine."

"That would be wonderful, Giovanni," Antonio replied.

Antonio led Maria to their table, took her coat, and pulled out her chair for her to sit before he went around and sat opposite her. Once seated, Giovanni came back with a chilled bottle of wine and opened it in front of them.

"Antonio, I have a nice'a bottle of 1928 Chateau Coutet, Barsac. I hope that it is'a to your liking."

Giovanni poured a little in their glasses for them to taste. Antonio and Maria both sipped the wine and then placed their glasses back on the table.

"What do you think, Maria?" asked Antonio.

"I think it is just fantastic. What year did you say it was from again?"

"It'sa from'a 1928. It'a was specially made'a, and shipped inside a case'a of mozzarella." Giovanni laughed.

"Giovanni, you are a great man of wine. Please bring us an antipasto for two to start with, and while you're getting that we can figure out what to order."

"That is'a very good, Antonio. I will be right'a back."

Giovanni went back to the kitchen as Maria and Antonio started to look over the menu.

"Antonio, what do you recommend?"

"Oh, let me see. Just about everything here is great, but one of my favorites is their chicken Marsala. It is to die for."

Maria chuckled. "Well, I don't want to die on our first date, Antonio."

"You're quick! I like that. Would you like some wine?"

"Yes please."

Antonio filled Maria's glass about three quarters of the way and did the same with his, then placed the bottle back in the ice to keep it chilled. At that moment Giovanni came from the kitchen with their antipasto and placed it in the middle of the table.

"There you go. I hope'a you enjoy it. Have'a you two decided what'a you want for dinner?"

"Maria?"

"Yes, Giovanni, Antonio here recommends your chicken Marsala, so I think I will go with that."

"I can'a guarantee you have'a not had any better. What'a would you like'a to order, Antonio?"

"Hmmm...I think tonight I will have spaghetti aglio e olio, heavy on the parmesan."

"Those are'a excellent choices. I will'a have it out'ta for you shortly."

"Thanks so much, Giovanni."

Giovanni headed back to the kitchen as Antonio and Maria started on their antipasto.

"I will tell you one thing...his cooking is a bit slow, but it is well worth the wait," Antonio said while he ate.

The two continued to eat their salads until Giovanni brought out their meals and placed them on the table in front of them.

"Here you two go. Eat'a well, my friends."

"Grazie, Giovanni."

"Yes, Giovanni, grazie."

They ate their meal and made small talk throughout. Once finished they drove back to Maria's apartment, and Antonio walked her to her apartment door.

"You know what, Maria? I have had a fantastic time. You are so different from most of the dames...I mean ladies...I have dated."

"You men and your labels! But I had a great time too."

Antonio leaned down and gave Maria a quick, but soft, kiss.

"Do you think we can go out again sometime soon?"

"I would like that, Antonio. I will see you again at the Eldorado for sure. We will have to go from there, because I don't always know my schedule."

"That would be fine. You have a great night."

Antonio waited until Maria was inside and then walked downstairs, got into his car, and drove away. Maria watched his every move and spit on the floor in anger.

"Oh, we will see a lot of each other. The fun has just begun. I am going to play you like a fiddle."

***

Antonio and Maria saw each other on a regular basis over the next few weeks. After a day at the horse races, where they had both done well on their wagers, Antonio took her for supper at a local Greek restaurant. After they finished their dessert Antonio led Maria to the car.

"Maria, we have been going out for some time now, and I was wondering if you would be interested in going with me to my place?"

"Oh, Antonio, if you are asking what I think you are, I am sorry. You see, I made a promise to God, my father, and my mother that I would save myself for the right man."

Antonio interrupted her as she spoke. "I thought that I was your guy?"

"Antonio, please, I need you to hear me out. I promised them that I would not give myself to any man until I got married. I have kept that promise so far...I hope you understand."

"You mean...?"

"Yes, silly. I am still a virgin, and I plan on staying that way until there is a band around my finger."

Antonio laughed. "You know I can't go against a promise to God, and surely not one to your mother. Forget I asked, okay? I hope that doesn't change things for us, because I am really liking what we have going here."

"Oh, we're fine. You want to bring me home, though? I may have had one too many mint juleps, and could use some rest."

"Not a problem. Let's head back."

***

After dating for many months, Antonio had fallen hard for Maria. All the while she hated his guts, but her game had to be played out...she had to get him right where she wanted him.

Chapter Six
The Game Takes the Next Step

A year after Maria and Antonio started dating, the two of them walked in Gromper's Park along the Chicago River. At sunset, Antonio led Maria to a park bench at the riverside and they both sat down. Antonio seemed very nervous to Maria, and she was startled when, all of a sudden, he slid off the bench and went down to one knee.

"Maria, we have been going together for over a year now, and I knew from the moment that I met you there was a connection between us. I need you to know that I love you with all my heart, and I want to spend the rest of my life with you. I guess what I am trying to say...." Antonio pulled a box out of his pocket and opened it before Maria, revealing a large diamond engagement ring. "Would you be my wife, and make me the happiest man in the world?"

"Antonio, I must say you have caught me off guard. I do love you, but I need to know that you're going to be around. The work you do with Mr. Bianchi frightens me, and if we were to have a family, I would want our children to have a father. Do you understand what I am saying?"

"I cannot promise you anything more than that I am working to get off the streets, and should be out of harm's way soon. Please say yes. I can't live without you in my life."

"Oh, Antonio, how can a girl say no to those beautiful brown eyes of yours? Yes, I will marry you."

Antonio took the ring out of the box and slipped it on the third finger of Maria's left hand. He then stood up and pulled Maria to her feet and into his arms, and they sealed the deal with a long, passionate kiss.

***

Six months later, both Maria's and Antonio's families and friends filled the pews of the Assumption Catholic Church, which was beautifully decorated with ribbons, bows, and flowers. Maria's best friend, Gianna Racan, was her maid-of-honor, and her three bridesmaids included her sister Theresa. Since her father was dead, Maria had asked Gianna's brother Johnny to walk her down the aisle and give her away.

Maria and Johnny were in the back room as they waited for the time to come.

"Maria, are you sure that you want to do this? I know of a couple of guys from high school who, for the right amount of money, would off the son of a bitch for you."

"Listen, Johnny, like everyone else you don't seem to understand. I am going to put this guy away. I don't want him dead...I want him to suffer for years and years, like Theresa and I have without my dad."

"I can understand how you feel. I just can't help but worry about you."

"Thanks, Johnny...you're a peach."

Gianna opened the door and walked into the room.

"Okay, young lady. Are you ready?"

"Ready as I have ever been."

"Okay, let's get into position."

The three of them walked out of the small room and lined up in the hallway.

At the same time, Antonio stood in the front by the altar with his best man, Jack Palermo. His groomsmen were all from Mr. Bianchi's mob family. He had chosen Joey Petriani, Jackie Marchetti, and Demetrio DeSilva to be his witnesses. They all stood with Father Constantino, who was to perform the ceremony.

First, the bridesmaids walked down the aisle, each escorted by a groomsman, and then Gianna and another groomsman followed. Everyone stood and all heads turned as Maria stood in the entryway with Johnny, and there was a collective gasp when they saw how beautiful she looked. The ring bearer and flower girl started down the aisle, and Maria stepped forward on Johnny's arm, looking like the happiest bride anyone had ever seen.

After Maria joined Antonio at the altar and Johnny had found his seat, Father Constantino performed mass first, and then he proceeded with the marriage ceremony of Antonio and Maria.

"Do you, Antonio Joseph Capresi, take Maria Louisa Cachiotti to be your lawfully wedded wife?"

"I do."

"Do you promise to love, honor, cherish, and protect her, forsaking all others and holding only unto her?"

"I do."

"Do you, Maria Louisa Cachiotti, take Antonio Joseph Capresi to be your lawfully wedded husband?"

"I do."

"Do you promise to love, honor, cherish, and protect him, forsaking all others and holding only unto him?"

"I do."

"Antonio, I need you to please repeat after me. I, Antonio Joseph Capresi, take thee, Maria Louisa Cachiotti."

"I, Antonio Joseph Capresi take thee, Maria Louisa Cachiotti."

"To have and to hold, in sickness and in health, for richer or poorer."

"To have and to hold, in sickness and in health, for richer or poorer," Anthony repeated.

"To love and cherish, from this day forward, until death do us part. With this ring, I thee wed," the priest continued to Anthony.

"To love and cherish, from this day forward, until death do us part. With this ring, I thee wed."

"Place the ring upon her hand."

Antonio took Maria's hand and put the ring on her finger.

The priest completed the vows with Maria, and then instructed her to place the ring on his hand.

"By the power vested in me by the Roman Catholic Church and the State of Illinois, I now pronounce you husband and wife. You may kiss your bride."

Antonio lifted up Maria's veil and gave her a passionate kiss, then they turned for the priest to present them to the congregation.

"I introduce to you, Mr. and Mrs. Antonio Capresi."

Antonio and Maria took each other's hand and walked down the aisle as everyone threw rice at them.

No one saw Maria's mother as she approached Father Constantino with a rosary in her hand.

"Father, please bless this special rosary for Maria. I am going to give it to her later."

"No problem, Mrs. Cachiotti." He took the rosary from Brigitta and raised it towards the cross at the front of the church. "Blessed be our God and Father, who has given us the mysteries of His Son to be pondered with devotion and celebrated with faith. May He grant us, His faithful people, who by praying the rosary we may, with Mary, the Mother of Jesus, seek to keep His joys, sorrows, and glories in our minds and hearts. We ask this through Christ our Lord. Amen."

Father Constantino turned and handed the rosary back to Brigitta.

"Thank you so much, Father. Will you come to the reception?"

"Yes, I wouldn't miss it. Although I may not care for some of the company that is going to be there, for you and Maria, I will be there."

"Thank you. See you there, Father."

***

Two hours later there were several hundred people at the reception at a large wine vineyard just south of Chicago, which included all of the Bianchi mob family. People were dancing and singing, while many stood around and ate from the large buffet that was laid out for the guests.

But not everyone was that involved in the festivities. Demetrio DeSilva, Joey Petriani, and Tony DeStephano stood away from the crowd and talked mob business.

"Hey, Joey, I heard that old man Caprino is acting up in your turf. What's the down low on that?"

"He is getting to be a thorn in my side. We had to let his boys know they aren't welcome in South Chicago, but they keep showing their ugly mugs."

"You know, if this was New York, Caprino would be wearing cement galoshes."

"Mr. Big man, huh, Tony? Well, I can't move on him until the Godfather himself tells me I can. Until then, we just keep pounding them."

Just as they finished, Pasquale Bianchi's personal consigliere Jackie Marchetti stood up in front of the crowd with his wife Camilla.

"Everyone, can I have your attention please? I would like for you all to stand and say a toast to the new couple."

The crowd turned to face Maria and Antonio, who were seated at the head table, and raised their glasses. Once a quiet had come over the crowd, Jackie continued.

"'Evviva Gli Sposi'! Long live the newlyweds! Okay, and now one from my lovely wife Camilla."

Camilla said, "'Vi sia crescere golden e avere tanti figli'! May you both grow golden and have many children." The crowd applauded and clanged on their glasses.

***

The music had begun to play again in the background as Maria walked around with a camera to get pictures of all of the Bianchi mobsters and Antonio's family. Everyone allowed their picture to be taken until she tried to capture Antonio and Pasquale Bianchi, who were in the corner talking. Mr. Bianchi turned away and grabbed Antonio by his arm.

"Antonio! What the hell is your wife trying to do? We don't need anyone taking our picture."

"Why not, Mr. Bianchi? She just wants pictures of everyone for her wedding album."

"Antonio, listen to me. It's just not good for business. Now go over and have her stop. Please."

"Okay, I will take care of it, Mr. Bianchi."

Antonio walked over to Maria and smiled.

"Maria, what are you doing? You're supposed to be having fun. Let the photographer take the pictures...that's what I'm paying him for. Please, just go back to the reception, and I will be right back."

"Okay, but please hurry back." Antonio walked back over to Mr. Bianchi.

"Sorry, Mr. Bianchi. We can talk inside if you like."

"Yes, I think that would be best."

Antonio followed Pasquale into the clubhouse and then to a sitting room, where Arabella Bianchi, Godfather Bianchi's wife, and Marisa DeSilva were seated.

Mr. Bianchi went to his wife. "Would you two ladies mind going outside? I need to speak to Antonio."

"That is not a problem, my husband. Marisa, let's go find Maria," said Arabella.

"I'm right behind you. We'll let the men talk. I need to freshen up my champagne anyway."

"Me too, and some dessert would be heavenly."

As the two ladies left the room, Mr. Bianchi sat down in a large, high backed chair.

"Antonio, please come on over here and have a seat."

Antonio sat down on the couch and faced Bianchi.

"Now, Antonio, how long have you been with me?"

"I guess ever since I was a kid running numbers back and forth. So, right about fourteen years, Mr. Bianchi."

"I have come to trust you, and you seem to have a good head on your shoulders. I need a favor from you."

Mr. Bianchi took a cigar from his jacket pocket and lit it.

"Would you like a cigar?"

"Yes, thank you, Mr. Bianchi. What would you like for me to do?"

Antonio stood up and walked over as Mr. Bianchi took out another cigar, handed it to him, and then lit it for him. Antonio then returned to his seat.

"I'm having a major problem out of Giovanni Caprino's area on the North side. They are constantly trying to move in on a couple of properties in our territory. I want to send a very important message to Giovanni."

"I can see where that would present a problem. What do you need me to do?"

"I am glad you can see that. So, my proposition to you is this. I need you to get close to the Caprino familia and put a hit on his son Stephano. He needs to get a nice Chicago overcoat. Now, I know this is a dangerous assignment, so if you take care of this for me, maybe I will move you up in the ranks. I could make you one of my capos. The money alone would be well worth it. What do you think?"

"I have no problem with doing that for you, Mr. Bianchi."

"That is very good, Antonio. When you do, take whomever you need to drive. Comprende?"

"Yes, sir, I fully understand. I will take Jack. He and I have worked together for a long time, and he knows how I prefer to do things."

"I want to know all the details after it is done. You make it happen after you get back from your honeymoon and I will take care of you and your wife.

Don't fail me. If you fail me, you won't have to worry about ever failing me again. Capiche?"

"I promise you, Mr. Bianchi, it will be taken care of."

"Very good…that is what I wanted to hear from you. Now, go find your wife and enjoy the rest of your reception."

Moments later Antonio exited the house and found Maria standing with Arabella and Marisa.

"Will you ladies please excuse me? I need to go grab my new husband."

Arabella replied laughingly. "Seems everyone needs to talk today, to everyone except us. That's our cue, Marisa."

Maria walked over to Antonio and met him away from everyone else.

"Antonio, what did Mr. Bianchi want?"

"Oh, it was nothing much babe, just business."

"Business…at our wedding?"

"Dollface, please. Let's just get back to the reception."

"I am just saying that I can't believe that you would be doing mob business at our reception."

"Just drop it, okay, Maria? Let's go and start opening all those gifts that we got."

"Okay, but no more business talks for today. Okay?"

"I promise."

"I love you!"

"I love you too, Maria."

The two newlyweds walked back to the head table and sat down to receive their guests who wanted to congratulate the new couple.

***

With the reception behind them, the two newlyweds got into the limousine and drove away to start their honeymoon.

"Hey, Antonio, you haven't told me where we are going on our honeymoon."

"You know what, you're right...I haven't."

"So are you going to tell me, silly?"

"Do I have too?"

"Please tell me where we are going."

"Okay. I hope you brought your bathing suit. We are going to a little place in Mexico called Cozumel."

"Yes, I brought it. Now I can't wait to get there!"

The newlyweds pulled up to the airport, and within moments were on a plane heading to their honeymoon. Once on the plane Maria's stomach began to churn as she fought off the anger she felt, while at the same time knowing what was to happen that evening. She was going to have to have sex with the very man that had killed her father. She knew she could never call it making love, because there was no love involved. This was going to be sex, plain and simple. Maria had to give her virginity to Antonio. He didn't deserve that honor, but in order to play the game out she had to make sure that he was totally unaware of what she was doing.

Once they landed in Cozumel, Antonio took her straight to the room. Maria unpacked the suitcases while Antonio stood out on the balcony smoking a cigar and drinking a glass of Scotch from their in-room bar. She then went out on the balcony and joined her husband.

"Antonio, do me a favor and pour me a glass of champagne?"

"Sure, doll, but do you want to drink before we go to supper?"

"Yeah...we are celebrating, aren't we?"

"You got me there. One sec and I will get it," Antonio said as he turned and faced her. He looked deeply into her eyes, took her face in his hands, and kissed her passionately. Maria returned the kiss as she had many times before.

Antonio opened a bottle of champagne and poured them both a glass. Returning to Maria on the balcony, he handed one of the drinks to her. "Maria, a toast. To us—may we have many beautiful years together, and love as long as time itself."

"Cheers," Maria said, placing the glass to her lips.

"Okay, enough with the drinks. I hope you are hungry, because I made reservations at the most renowned five-star restaurant in the area."

"I am ready to eat. Can I go freshen up my makeup?"

"Sure, dollface, you have plenty of time. Go do your thing and then we will go."

Maria went to the bathroom and stared into the mirror. She knew what this was all leading up to, and it almost made her want to vomit, but she was locked in. There was no turning back now. She had to play it through no matter what it took. She fixed her makeup, and then the two of them went downstairs to the front of the hotel. There they took a horse-drawn surrey around town before stopping at a beautiful restaurant called Sammy's Place.

After they had dinner they went dancing, and Maria had a few drinks. In fact, she had planned to get a little tipsy, because she knew she could never handle what was to come if she was sober.

***

Antonio could see that she'd had a little too much. It was also eleven o'clock, and Antonio was more than ready to consummate the marriage…he had been ready since the first time he'd seen her.

"Hey, sweetheart, how about we head back to the room? I think we both have had enough drinking and dancing."

"Okay, you silly little man. Take away all the fun." Maria laughed as Antonio twisted her around on the dance floor.

The two dancers left the floor and Antonio helped Maria with her fur jacket. They stepped outside where a limo was waiting for them. The driver came around and opened the door for them and they got inside.

Once at the hotel, Antonio paid the driver and they quickly went upstairs. Once inside their suite, Antonio stopped Maria in the middle of the room and held her close.

"You know, Maria, I just have to say that I love you with all my heart. I hope that I can be the man you have always dreamed of having." Then he kissed her with all the raw emotion he could muster.

"I love you too, Antonio. You will need to be gentle with me tonight, as I have never done this before."

"Oh, babe, I promise."

"Let me go to the bathroom and change into something a bit more befitting the moment."

"Take your time, babe. I will be on the balcony."

***

Maria went into the bathroom and changed into a sexy, slinky silk nightgown that Mr. Bianci's wife had given her as a gift at the bridal shower. She fixed her makeup and then stared at the mirror.

"You got this. Just go with the flow, because it is only sex. Someday, after this piece of trash is gone, you will find a real man."

Maria walked into the living room and cleared her throat to get Antonio's attention. He turned around immediately, and couldn't seem to keep his mouth from dropping open when he saw how beautiful Maria looked. She was a full figured girl, with everything in the right places.

"Oh Lord, an angel just fell from Heaven," Antonio said as he made his way into the room.

"Now, Antonio, please take your time. I have never done this before."

"Don't worry, babe. We have all night."

Antonio began to disrobe, and he took Maria by the hand and led her into the bedroom. He looked down at Maria's hands when they began to shake.

"Relax, Maria. I will be gentle."

"Thank you…I need to just calm down. Maybe a glass of champagne?"

"Sure, doll. Why don't you go make yourself comfortable, and I will be right back."

Maria climbed into bed while Antonio went to pour the champagne. When he returned and handed it to her, she sipped at it, trying to draw some courage from the bubbles.

Finally, Maria placed the glass on the bedside table, and Antonio climbed into the bed.

"I love you with all my heart, Maria."

"I love you too."

The two had sex, and when finished, Antonio sat on the edge of the bed.

"I hope I was not too rough, Maria."

"You were great, my husband. I never knew what I was missing out on. You are the perfect lover," Maria lied as she lay there feeling disgusted.

"Thank you, doll. This is the first night of the rest of our lives."

"I know, and what a wonderful life it will be."

Maria climbed out of bed and went to the bathroom to freshen up, and Antonio put on a bathrobe and went out onto the balcony.

G. R. Holton & Marlene Mendoza

Chapter Seven
Antonio Makes His First Mistake

Antonio and Maria returned from their honeymoon three weeks later, and Antonio spent the entire next week watching Stephano and tracking his every move. At the end of the week Antonio and Jack Palermo were in Antonio's Studebaker, across the street from Chicago's famous Normandy House, as Stefano Caprino and a female came out. The couple walked down the street on the sidewalk, and as they walked along, Jack slowly followed them with the car for two blocks and then crossed the street to get behind them.

"Okay, Jack, pull over so that I can get out."

Antonio got out of the car and quickly moved up close behind Stephano, then pulled out his gun and stuck it into the small of Stephano's back.

"Okay you two, into the alley," Antonio whispered so as not to attract any attention.

Both Stephano and his girl walked down the alleyway, but suddenly Stephano stopped and turned to face his foe. Antonio was five feet away, with his pistol pointed to the area between Stephano's eyes.

"Okay, just who the hell are you? My father is the godfather around here, and I have plenty of green. Let me get to my wallet and you can have it all!" Stephano yelled.

"Who I am is of no consequence. I appreciate the offer Stephano, but I don't want your money. See, it seems that Mr. Bianchi is very unhappy about how your father is doing business."

"How the hell do you know my name? Just who the hell are you anyway?"

Antonio looked at the woman, who was now cowering behind Stephano.

"Like I told you, my name is unimportant. Young lady, first off I wouldn't be standing behind Stephano unless you want to be an unlucky bystander, and secondly, I am going to let you go. When I do, you need to go back to Mr. Caprino and tell him that it would be in his best interests to stay out of the South side. Stephano, it is time for your big kiss off."

"Listen, don't do this. Whatever Mr. Bianchi is paying you, I can triple it and make you a capo."

"You have nothing to offer me. Now young lady, get out of here."

The girl stepped quickly away from Stephano. Just as she did Antonio fired twice. The bullets hit Stephano between the eyes and in his forehead. The female screamed and ran out of the alley just as Stephano fell to the ground.

Antonio walked quickly out of the alley and through the crowd that was forming in the alley opening. Jack pulled up and Antonio jumped into the car. The tires squealed as they hastily left the area. Once they were clear, Antonio turned and tapped Jack on the shoulder.

"Hey, Jack, let's go get a drink...I could use a shot and a beer. But first, take a quick run by the river so I can get rid of this piece."

"That sounds good to me. Where do you want to go?"

"Let's get out of the area for a bit. Maybe we could go down to the burlesque club outside of town."

"You got it."

Jack drove the car until they were at a very secluded area of the Chicago River. Antonio got out, walked to the river's edge, and then tossed the murder weapon far out into the water. Without a second's hesitation he turned and jumped back into the car.

"Okay, we are all set. Let's go get that drink," Antonio said as he closed the door.

"You got it."

Jack turned the car around and headed further south until they reached Curley's Burlesque. As they entered, a beautiful blonde was dancing on a pole, and several redheads and brunettes were mingling with the customers. The place was loaded with truckers, since it was right off the main highway.

After having a few drinks and a few lap dances, Antonio had Jack take him home so he could have supper with Maria. He took off his jacket and went into the kitchen, where Maria was cooking.

"Hey, babe, did you have a good day?" asked Maria.

"Nothing out of the ordinary. Will supper be long?"

"No, it is almost ready. Why don't you go wash up, and it will be on the table in a few minutes?"

"Great, because I am starved."

Antonio washed his hands in the bathroom then took off his shirt and walked out into the dining room in his slacks and t-shirt. The two of them ate supper, then Maria cleared the table.

"Antonio, do you want any dessert? I baked a nice rhubarb pie."

"Yeah, I will have some, and coffee too if you don't mind baby."

"I don't mind at all."

Antonio finished his dessert quickly and retired to the living room to read the newspaper he had brought home.

***

A couple of hours later Antonio and Maria were lying in bed. Maria was reading a book when Antonio turned to face her.

"Maria, I need you to do something for me."

"What's that?"

"If you are ever asked by anyone where I was today, you tell them that we were out shopping for furniture. Okay?"

"Why? Where did you go? What did you do this time?"

"I am going to say this once. Don't ever ask any questions. It is better you don't know. If there is something that I need you to know, I will tell you. Just do as I say. Okay?"

"You know I don't like this mob stuff. When will it all stop? We need to have a stable family, where I don't have to worry that you are going to be shot at all the time."

"Don't worry about that, Maria. Mr. Bianchi is giving me a new position. I won't be on the streets much longer, promise, and then maybe we can begin to plan that family you want."

"Well, that's all fine, but I think we should just leave this area and forget the mob."

"Now, Maria, you should know that it's not that easy. Mr. Bianchi takes great care of us and deserves our respect. Now, get some sleep and remember what I said. We spent the day shopping for furniture, and that is all."

"Okay, but I don't have to like it."

Antonio rolled back over and turned out his light.

***

The next morning, Maria put Antonio's breakfast on the table in front of him, then walked over and sat in her seat. It was easy to see that she was still a bit upset about the previous night's conversation.

"I am sorry for being so gruff last night. There are things that go on in the business that you are better off not knowing. The less you know means less trouble for both of us."

"If it has anything to do with my house and family, though, I think I have a right to know."

"Babe, just remember that I was with you all day yesterday and we will be fine."

"I don't like it, but you are my husband and I will do as you ask."

"Okay, thank you. Now, I will be late tonight. Mr. Bianchi has some business he wants to talk to me about."

"It seems that lately you are never home at night. I wish you'd let me go back to singing at the club so I wouldn't get so lonely."

"Like I said…business. And no wife of mine is gonna work in a dive like that…end of discussion."

Antonio got up from the table, kissed Maria goodbye, then grabbed his coat and walked out.

"Business my ass. I know that you're up to something. One of these days I will have you right where I want you."

***

Later that day, Maria was standing at the newsstand looking at the new edition of Time Magazine. She glanced over and the newspaper headline caught her eye.

"Oh my God! 'Stephano Caprino, the son of a suspected mob boss, was shot in cold blood outside the Normandy Restaurant.' That's where he was. I knew there was something up when he told me to lie about where he was yesterday. He killed this guy and wants me to cover his ass. Well, Antonio, you did me a favor by warning me. I never would have known, and now you have made your first big mistake."

Maria paid for a copy of the paper and then quickly walked away from the stand with it tucked under her arm. Once home she went directly to her bedroom, got down on her knees, and pulled up the small rug beside her bed. Using a screwdriver, she pried up a loose board, then reached into the hole and removed a black notebook. She cut out the newspaper article about the shooting with a pair of scissors, then placed the clipping in the back of the notebook. Retrieving a pencil off the nightstand, she began to write in the book, reading it aloud as she wrote.

"Okay, let's see. 'August 27th, 1935. Antonio makes like a ghost for the afternoon and tells me that I have to lie about where he was; then Stephano Caprino is found shot to death at the same time.' One more nail in your coffin, you son of a bitch."

Maria placed the notebook back into the hole, replaced the board, and then pulled the rug back over it. She then got up and quickly took the rest of the newspaper out the front door to dump it in the garbage shoot.

"I don't need Antonio finding this in the apartment. He would definitely wonder why I bought the paper, and why the front page was missing. I really don't need him getting suspicious. It is way too early in this game."

***

Several days later, Maria visited the cemetery where her father was buried. In the distance, she could see the Caprino family gathered for Stephano's funeral. Tears ran down her face as she knelt down and placed fresh roses on her father's grave.

"Papa, I am getting closer and closer. Someday soon I will avenge your death. One day Mr. Bianchi and any other mobster I can find dirt on will go down, and Antonio will either die or spend the rest of his decrepit life behind bars. I made you that promise, and I plan to keep it."

Maria got up, dusted the dirt off her dress, and walked away.

Chapter Eight
Things Begin To Heat Up

A week later, Mr. Bianchi, Arabella, Antonio, Jackie, and Joey all sat around the desk in Mr. Bianchi's office. Mr. Bianchi sat behind his desk.

"Arabella, could you please go get some vino for the boys?"

"Sure, honey, I'll be right back."

Arabella got up from her chair beside her husband's desk and left the room. Mr. Bianchi then began to inform the rest of the group of some changes to operations.

"Okay, now, this is how it's going to work. Antonio, you have won favor with me. You took care of Stephano for me, and I made you a promise. Joey, I want you to take Antonio under your wing and show him what you do. You both are now my caporegimes for the South Chicago area. Joey will handle the east side and Antonio the west. You have any problem with that, Joey?"

"Whatever you feel is best, Mr. Bianchi."

"I am honored, Mr. Bianchi, and I will do my very best. I don't want to step on Joey's toes, though."

"You aren't stepping on my toes, Antonio. I always want what is best for the business, and you will make a fine capo if you listen to me."

"Thanks, Joey."

Mr. Bianchi took a cigar from his humidor. "I know you will become an asset as my capo, Antonio, and Joey is fine with it. Now, let's get down to the business I have called you all here about. It seems that a few New York City businesses have fallen quite behind since the depression started. But that is not my problem...I really don't care what their excuses are. Jackie, I want you to take a few of our boys to New York and meet up with Tony DeStephano. Find out who these loafers are and take care of things. You tell Tony that if he can't run things, then I will find someone that can!"

"You got it boss. I will leave tomorrow and take Jack Palermo and Vinny Couture with me."

"Okay, very good. Antonio, I have a job for you to do. I need you to take this envelope and meet up with Mayor David Fogerty down at the Lamp Lighter Lounge tomorrow at noon. I want you to take your time with this meeting, have some lunch with him, and above all else make sure that absolutely no one sees the exchange."

Mr. Bianchi handed an envelope to Antonio, which Antonio placed in his inner suit jacket pocket.

"I will do it just as you ask, Mr. Bianchi."

"That is all I have for now. You all can go."

Each man approached Mr. Bianchi and kissed his ring before they left the room.

***

Antonio was reading the paper as Maria took his suit jacket to put with the rest of the dry cleaning. She reached inside the inner pocket and pulled out the envelope meant for the mayor.

"Antonio, what the hell is this?"

Antonio got up and snatched the envelope out of Maria's hand.

"It is none of your concern."

"If it is in my house it is my concern. What is going on?"

Before she even saw it coming, Antonio raised his hand and backhanded Maria in the mouth. A trickle of blood rolled down her lip, but Maria just wiped her mouth and glared at him.

"You no good son of a bitch! To use your words, I am going to tell you this just once...don't you ever lay a hand on me again!"

"I'm sorry that I lost my temper, dollface. Listen...everything I do is strictly for the business."

"I don't care about your business. You ever lay a hand on me again and you will wake up a very unhappy man."

"Boy, one smack and now you're a cocky broad. You would be best off not making threats. Now go make me some coffee."

"I swear, one of these days, Antonio, that stuff will catch up to you."

"Whatever…now just go make my coffee and shut up."

As Antonio walked into the living room, Maria went into the kitchen, whispering to herself.

"I swear I will make you pay for that!"

***

The next morning, Antonio entered the kitchen dressed in his best suit. He sat down to drink his coffee and Maria was still at the stove.

"Hey, muffin, I am really sorry about what happened between us last night. There are just things you are better off not knowing. I don't know why I lost my temper, and I promise to never do it again."

"I just worry about what you're getting yourself into."

"I know, but business is just that…business. By the way, don't hold supper tonight. I will be out late."

"Where are you going this time?"

"There you go again! You ask way too many questions, Maria. I will be late, that is all."

Antonio finished his coffee, got up from his seat, and walked out of the apartment. Maria watched out the window as he got into his car and drove away. As soon as he was out of sight she picked up the phone and called her best friend Gianna Racan. The phone rang a couple of times before Gianna finally answered it.

"Hello, this is Gianna."

"Hey, Gianna, this is Maria. I need a favor really bad."

"What do you need, sweetie?"

"I need Antonio followed. He is up to no good, and it may be another woman. Do you know anyone that could help me out?"

"Yeah, let me get my brother. He can help, and he would keep his mouth shut too."

"Great! Antonio just took off and said he won't be home for dinner. But he usually hangs out at the Eldorado Club. If there is any way that Johnny could do this for me I would really appreciate it. I know Johnny gave me away at the wedding, and I'm a little concerned that Antonio might recognize him and get suspicious. Please just ask him to stay far enough away not to be seen, and to get pictures of what the snake is doing."

"No problem, dear. I just hate the way he treats you."

"I hate it too. Would you believe last night he hit me in the mouth because I asked about an envelope that was in his suit?"

"You are kidding me! Are you sure you want to keep this game going on any further? He will kill you if he finds out what you are doing."

"I am going through with this no matter what. After last night I am even more certain. I warned him that if he does it again he will wake up very unhappy."

"That is great. Don't let him get away with that kind of crap. I will get with my brother and get a tag put on that son of a bitch. Okay, girl, if that is what you want."

"Thanks, you're a dear. Well, I need to go to town and do some shopping. I will talk to you later on. Let me know what your brother says."

"I will, sweetie, ciao."

Maria hung up the phone and went to the bedroom. She took the notebook out of its hiding place and added all of the information about the envelope and Antonio hitting her.

"He is digging himself in deeper and deeper. Sooner or later he will dig himself all the way to Hell."

***

At the same time Gianna picked up the phone and called her brother Johnny. After a few rings Johnny Racan picked up.

"Hey, this is Gianna. Got a sec?"

"Yeah, what do you need?"

"I need you to help out a friend of mine who has hubby problems."

"Who is it?"

"You know Maria?"

"Of course I do...I gave her away, silly. What's up?"

"Well, you know that Antonio is tied in with the mob and is gone all the time. She needs to know what he is up too. But you have to be quiet about it."

"Oh yeah, I know him. He is a real piece of work, but you know how much I hate the mob. Tell her I will see what I can do. I have got to run. I'll talk to you later."

"Thanks, Johnny. Give me a ring tonight."

***

At lunchtime, Antonio left the Eldorado Club and got into his car. Johnny Racan was across the street in his car watching Antonio's every move. When Antonio pulled out, Johnny started the engine of his car and put it in gear.

"Okay, you son of a bitch, let's just see what you're up too."

Johnny followed Antonio's car to the Lamp Lighter Lounge. Johnny parked his car in an inconspicuous spot as Antonio got out and went into the building. All the while Johnny took pictures of his every move.

***

Antonio walked in the door and saw David Fogerty sitting in a booth in the back of the room. He walked down the aisle and stopped in front of the mayor and the chief of police.

"Good afternoon, Mr. Mayor; and you too, Chief."

The chief stood up and put his hand on his gun. "And just who the hell are you?"

"My name is Antonio Capresi. I have something for you, Mr. Mayor, from Mr. Bianchi."

"Please have a seat."

"Wait. Before you sit down I want your heater," the chief stated.

"Hey, I don't give up the piece!"

"Give it up or walk."

"Chief, you're an ass."

"As usual. But give me the gun."

Antonio finally handed his gun to the chief and then sat down across from the two of them.

"Antonio, what can I get you to drink?"

"Just a glass of red wine would do just fine."

"Waitress, get us a bottle of your finest Nebbiolo."

"Why, thank you, Mr. Mayor."

As the waitress turned to face the bar Antonio took the envelope out of his pocket and slid it over to the mayor. The mayor took the envelope and quickly placed it into his jacket pocket.

"Antonio, I want you to let Mr. Bianchi know that everything is taken care of with this donation to my re-election campaign."

"I am taken care of also. He will have no trouble out of me." The chief gave him a knowing look.

"I know that Mr. Bianchi will be very pleased to hear that."

The waitress brought over the bottle of red wine and three wine glasses and set them on the table. The mayor filled the glasses, and as the men took their glasses, he made a toast.

"A toast to us. May it be a long and prosperous venture!"

"Grazie."

"Why don't we order something to eat? I hear they have a mean Reuben sandwich here."

"That sounds perfect, Mr. Mayor."

***

After about an hour, Mayor Fogerty and Antonio left the restaurant, shook hands, and went their separate ways, all of which Johnny documented on film. Johnny followed Antonio's car back to Bianchi's mansion, but kept going as there were many Bianchi soldiers at the main gate.

***

Days later Maria, Gianna, and Johnny all sat in Maria's living room discussing the meeting between Antonio and the mayor.

"Wow, these are really great pictures, Johnny. You're quite the photographer."

"No problem, Maria, but you better put them up before Antonio gets home."

"Yeah, you don't need him walking in and seeing what we have on him."

"That's the last thing I need. I am far from done with that son of a bitch, and the whole Bianchi family. They are going to pay for the day they killed my father. Sit here, I will be right back."

Maria left the room.

"Johnny, is there any chance you could get one of your friends to help watch Antonio without him knowing?"

"Well, let me think for a second. Hey, you know what? I could talk to Danny Donovan. He is actually a private investigator, and he owes me a big favor."

Just then Maria entered the room.

"Maria, Johnny here has a friend that can help keep an eye on Antonio. If he is doing anything wrong, he will know."

"Really? That would be fantastic! I need to know what he is doing. He is gone every day and coming in so late at night."

"Danny is a professional, so if anybody can get dirt on him, he can."

"Thank you so much, Johnny. I'm just so tired of him coming and going at all kinds of weird hours."

"No problem. I can't stand the mob anyway, and neither can Danny. Those mobsters just keep on taking, and if you don't do things their way you end up in a Chicago overcoat."

"Well, I want you and your friend to be careful. Just keep me informed. If you get anything, call Gianna and then have her call me, but only around noon. Antonio is never here then."

"Okay, you got it kiddo. Well, Gianna and I need to get going. My wife is patiently waiting for me at home to take her to the baby doctor."

"I pray all is well."

"She is doing fine, so it should be a quick visit. I will talk with you again soon. Let's go, Gianna."

"See ya later, Maria. How about doing lunch next Wednesday?"

"You got it. I'll see you then."

***

Late the next afternoon, Johnny and Danny Donovan sat at Johnny's kitchen table discussing Antonio and what needed to be done.

"Okay, so here is the deal, Danny. This is a picture of the guy."

Danny picked up the picture that Johnny slid across the table and checked it out.

"What I can tell you is this guy is as dirty as the day is long. I need to know what he is up to. Can you help me out?"

"You know that I am the best. Let me see what I can do. I don't like messing with the mob, but I know I owe you after all the help you gave my family when we needed it."

"I really appreciate you stepping up and helping us out. If all goes well there will be one less mob family to worry about. Just get me anything you can."

Danny got up and headed toward the door.

"Let's see what I can dig up. Give me a couple of days and I'll give you a call."

"Okay, just let me know."

Danny walked out the door and Johnny picked up the phone to call Maria. The phone rang a couple times before she picked up.

"Hello, this is Maria."

"Hey, Maria, this is Johnny. I got my friend on the job so we should hear back from him in a couple days."

"That is great. Just tell Gianna to call me when you're ready. I would prefer you didn't call at this time of day in case Antonio shows up and picks up the phone."

"I got ya, kiddo. I'll make sure to do that."

"Great. Talk to you soon. I really appreciate all that you are doing."

"No problem. See ya later alligator."

Johnny hung up the phone. "Boy, this guy is going to go down."

***

Around nine o'clock the following evening Antonio and Mr. Bianchi were in a corner booth at the Eldorado Club while Danny Donovan sat at the end of the bar. Danny drank his beer and tried to listen to the conversation between the other two.

"Antonio, it seems that we have a little problem. I hear from the streets that old man Colombo is back up to his old tricks. A couple of boys went there this morning and he is refusing to pay his insurance again. This has happened way too many times."

"I know, Mr. Bianchi. I guess he forgot what we did to his worker years ago. I have talked to the boys, but wanted to get your blessing before I let them loose."

"You have my blessing. This old man has been a thorn in my side for too many years. You do what you see is fitting."

"I will personally go and pay a visit to him."

"That is fine by me. Let me know when he is taken care of."

"I will, Mr. Bianchi."

"So how is married life treating you, Antonio?"

"Well, to be totally honest, I don't know. She really doesn't like what I am doing."

"Have you explained to her that she wouldn't have a pot to piss in if it wasn't for my generous salary?"

"I have, but you know women."

"The good news, Antonio, is that Arabella was against me working for the mob at first too. That was until I became a capo, and then underboss, and now the godfather."

"Yeah, she will come around I am sure. But in the meantime I think that blonde dish at the bar needs a little attention."

"You and the dames…they will be the death of you someday," Mr. Bianchi laughed.

"Oh, but Mr. Bianchi, what a way to die. I will talk to you soon, sir."

Antonio got up and approached the young, blonde haired beauty, who happened to be sitting two seats over from Danny.

"Hey, blondie, are you sitting here all alone?"

"Yeah. It's Sarah, Sarah Johnson. What about you?"

"You can call me Antonio. Why don't you come over and join me in a booth so that we can talk? What are you drinking?"

"Sure, sounds good to me. I'm drinking a cosmopolitan."

"Hey, bartender, I'll have one Scotch neat and a cosmopolitan for the lady. Bring it over to my table."

"Yes, sir, Mr. Capresi."

The bartender turned to make the drinks as Antonio took Sarah's hand and led her to his table. The bartender then brought the drinks over as Antonio and Sarah sat and laughed.

"Here you go, Mr. Capresi. Will there be anything else?"

"No, that's all for now."

"Very well, Mr. Capresi."

The bartender walked away from the table and went back behind the bar.

"Is everyone always so formal with you? What are you, some kind of politician or something?"

"I guess you could say that, or something close to it. What about you? What do you do?"

"Right now I'm trying to break into acting while I work as a waitress across town. I have always dreamed of being on stage, and one of these days I'm going to make it."

"Are you any good?"

Sarah grinned. "I would say that I am very good at many different things."

"I tell you what. I have some connections at the theater. If you stick with me, I will see what I can do about getting you in for an interview."

"That would be great, Mr. Capresi."

"Just call me Antonio, okay? Tell you what. Let's finish our drinks and go for a little ride to my place. I want to see if you're as good as you say you are."

"Sounds like a plan to me." Danny followed discreetly as they got up, left the club, and got into Antonio's car.

***

Danny got into his car and followed Antonio to an apartment complex on the west side of Chicago. He began to take pictures of the two of them as they got out of the car and walked up the stairs, stopping at the door for a passionate kiss. He also took pictures of the address on the outside of the building.

"Oh, this was just way too friggin' easy! Now I'll just sit here and wait," Danny said, laughing. Settling in for his stakeout, he noted the times he saw the apartment light turning off and on.

***

Moments later Antonio and Sarah walked into the spare apartment that Antonio kept to pick up women. Antonio took off his jacket and threw it on the couch, then went to the bar.

"Would you like a drink?"

"No thanks. I just need the ladies room to freshen up a bit."

"Yeah, sure, dollface, it's the second door on the left."

Sarah walked into the bathroom as Antonio poured himself a Scotch from the bar. When Sarah came out, the two of them met in the middle of the room and started to kiss passionately. Antonio led her by the hand to the bedroom, where they began to disrobe each other while they continued kissing, moving on to sex as soon as they were naked.

***

Little did Antonio know that the whole time they were in the apartment, Danny was in his car snapping pictures with a special lens, which took very detailed pictures. He had pictures of their shadows in the window, which were so clear there would be no doubt that it was Antonio and Sarah.

***

A few hours had passed. Antonio and Sarah were still in bed as Sarah ran her fingers through Antonio's chest hair.

"Muffin, you said you were good at many things, and I have to agree with you."

"Well, I never tell a lie, Antonio."

"It's getting late. I think we'd better get dressed and I will take you home."

"I agree about the time. I need to get home. I am working first thing in the morning and need my beauty rest."

"I don't think you could get any more beautiful than you already are. Tell you what. Give me your phone number and I will give you a call in a couple days after I talk to my friends at the theater."

"You're sweet, and I really appreciate it. I hope they can get me in for a tryout."

The two lovers came out of the front of the apartment complex and Antonio opened the door to the car for Sarah. She kissed him again as she got into the car.

***

Danny didn't miss any of this action with his camera, taking pictures of their every move. Deciding to call it a night, Danny packed up his camera and pulled away from the curb. "Oh this is way too good. He is dead meat."

The following morning Danny continued his surveillance. Before long, Antonio came out of the apartment and headed downtown, with Danny right on his trail. Antonio drove right to Colombo's Hardware store and parked out front. Danny watched intently as Antonio walked into the store.

***

There were a few people shopping, so Antonio pulled Guiseppi Colombo to the back of the store.

"Mr. Colombo, it has come to our attention that you are still refusing to pay your insurance."

"I told'a you a long'a time ago, I cannot'a pay what I don'ta have. Business is'a very slow right'a now, and I can't afford'a to pay Mr. Bianchi."

"You can't afford not to pay him. I tell you what. I am a generous man, so I am going to give you one more day. If you don't pay by tomorrow then I will have no choice but to come back and take care of you personally."

"Okay, okay. I will have'a the money by tomorrow. Just leave'a my store."

"I will be back tomorrow, and you better have the money. Got it?"

Antonio walked out the door.

***

That same day Maria and her sister Theresa were sitting in Maria's living room on the couch as they talked and drank tea.

"Maria, Mom and I are really getting nervous about this game you are playing with Antonio and the mob. You could get yourself killed if they ever find out what is really going on."

"I know, sis, but you didn't see Papa's face the day they shot him. I did. I swore a promise to him that they would pay for what they did to him, and I am going to make sure I keep that promise."

"Why don't you just turn in what you have? Afterwards you, me, and Momma will just pack up and leave. We can move to the west coast, and change our names if we have to. They will never find us."

Maria jumped up from the couch in frustration and stood in the middle of the room, crying as she yelled.

"You just don't understand! They killed our father...don't you even care?"

"I have learned to live with the idea that he is gone. Maybe you should too. We have to move on with our lives, Maria, before we don't have any lives to live."

Theresa got up, walked over to Maria, and hugged her.

"I am going to be fine. I have a professional private investigator now, and he is taking care of business. Trust me, everything will be okay."

"It's not you that I don't trust. It is the rest of those mobsters and what they are capable of."

The two girls hugged and a tear ran down Maria's face.

Chapter Nine
Another Man Dead

Bright and early the next morning Danny drove to a quiet spot far enough from Mr. Bianchi's house to remain undetected, but close enough to use a special telephoto lens so he could get pictures of anyone that came and went. From his car he also took pictures of the Bianchi house as mob soldiers stood outside the gate. As he watched, a long black car approached, passed through the gate unchallenged, and pulled up to the front of the house. Antonio exited his Studebaker and walked into the house.

***

Moments later Antonio, Jackie Marchetti, and Mr. Bianchi sat together in the office discussing Antonio's plans for Guiseppi Colombo.

"Antonio, I need you to take a couple of the boys over to Colombo's place today and finish this. I have grown tired of his refusals to pay me what he owes, and it is time to end it."

"I visited him yesterday and let him know that I would be back this morning, and that he better have your money."

"I want this over. No more chances for him…you will take a couple of guys and finish this, today. Capiche?"

"Okay, I will grab Jack and Vinny. I will take care of Colombo personally."

"Antonio, you just make sure that this can't come back on us," Jackie said as he stood next to Mr. Bianchi's desk.

Antonio walked over and stood face to face with Jackie.

"Jackie, I will do my job as usual. You just worry about yours."

"All I am saying is I don't want you to be sloppy with this."

Antonio pushed Jackie's shoulder.

"What makes you think I won't handle this the right way? I have always done my job, and it has always been clean."

Mr. Bianchi stood up from his chair and slammed his fist on the desk. "Okay, that is enough! Antonio, just go and do this. Afterwards I want you to come back here, as you and I have something very important to talk about."

"Yes sir."

Antonio walked out the library doorway and saw Jack Palmero and Vinny Couture standing guard by the front doorway.

"Okay you two, we have a job to do. Come with me."

"Sure thing, Mr. Capresi, right with you," Vinny replied.

The three walked out the front door and got in Antonio's 1925 Studebaker. Once they pulled out through the gate, they did not notice Danny Donovan as he followed them all the way to Colombo's Hardware. Once there Antonio and the other two men got out of the car and walked up to the door of the hardware store.

"Okay, you two. Just stand by and make sure no one comes into the store."

"You got it, boss."

Antonio walked into the store as the two other thugs stood on each side of the doorway outside. Antonio walked around the store to make sure that no one was there besides him and Mr. Colombo. He then went right to Colombo.

"Well, well, well, Mr. Colombo. Do you have Mr. Bianchi's money?"

"I don'ta have it all. This is'a all I have."

Antonio opened the envelope Mr. Colombo handed him, counted the money, and began to laugh.

"Guiseppi, what am I going to do with you? This must be some kind of a joke, right? This is nowhere near what you owe Mr. Bianchi. He's not going to be a happy man at all."

"I don'ta care," Mr. Colombo yelled as he spat on Antonio's shoes. "I'a pay when I can, and right'a now business is'a very slow. I barely have'a the money to pay my bills. You tell'a you boss that when I have'a the money, I will'a pay him."

"Well, that is not good enough. Mr. Bianchi has given you way too many chances, and you have displeased him for the last time."

Antonio took out his pistol and pointed it at Mr. Colombo's head. As Mr. Colombo saw the pistol and realized what was happening, he started to back away with a terrified look on his face.

"Please, I have a family to take care of—"

"That is not my problem. Good night, Mr. Colombo."

Antonio fired two shots into Colombo's forehead and he fell to the floor. A puddle of blood pooled behind Colombo's head as he lay on the floor. Antonio turned and ran out of the store.

***

Danny heard the shots as they rang out.

"Holy shit! They offed Mr. Colombo."

His camera was snapping as he heard the shots ring out and as Antonio ran out of the store. Stunned, Danny kept shooting pictures of Antonio and the two men as they got into the car, squealing tires as they took off from the scene.

***

Antonio yelled at his men. "Okay, boys, we need to get out of here, and quick. It won't take the cops long to get here since the station is right down the road."

"Okay, boss. We got ya."

***

Meanwhile, a large crowd formed in front of the store, and moments later the police pulled up.

"I need to get out of here before the coppers start asking me questions. I don't need to drop Antonio yet, as that would screw things up for Maria."

Danny set down his camera and slowly drove away.

***

An hour later, Antonio and the guys pulled up to Mr. Bianchi's house and stepped out of the vehicle.

"Okay, boys, put the car in the garage and go somewhere for a while. Get your alibis straight. I have to talk to Mr. Bianchi."

"Not a problem, boss," Jack replied as he got back into the car.

Antonio walked into the house and directly to Mr. Bianchi's office, where Jackie Marchetti, Mr. Bianchi, and Tony DeStephano all sat. Antonio walked to Mr. Bianchi's desk.

"Welcome back, Antonio. Did you take care of our little problem?" Mr. Bianchi said as he lit a cigar.

"Yes, sir. Mr. Colombo will no longer be an issue. I am sure that his son David will pay every bit of the money owed plus interest, or he gets the same treatment."

"Okay, very good. Now that you are here, Antonio, I have an important mission that involves you."

"Sure thing, Mr. Bianchi."

"Okay, have a seat." Mr. Bianchi got up from behind his desk and paced back and forth. "Here is my problem. It seems some of those damn Negros from

Harlem are trying to corner the heroin market. I haven't wanted to get involved with the drug trade, but it seems that they are stepping on our toes and moving into my territory. So, I have two choices: I either wipe them out, or we make a deal. At this point, I think that if we can get a piece of the action it would be more profitable than taking on the drug lords."

"I must say Mr. Bianchi, we do have a strong relationship with the judge and mayor in that area, and they should be able to give us some assistance. But being your consigliere, I do think that we really have to be cautious with this. Those Negros are very dangerous and could cause us much grief," Jackie countered.

Mr. Bianchi slammed his fist down on his desk. "I am not worried about grief! If they won't work with us willingly, then I will have no choice but to take out the leaders and control the market myself!"

Mr. Bianchi sat back down behind his desk.

"Now, this is what I want done. Antonio, you will go to New York City and work with Tony to get a meeting with their leaders. You will be acting on my behalf. I want fifteen percent of the action, and we will provide them all of the insurance that they need to keep the law off their back. We have the mayor already paid off and some of the police force. Let them know that we have the manpower to help them, and that this is not a deal to be taken lightly. This is to be productive and not just a trip for biscuits."

"I fully understand. But what if they don't want to deal?"

"Antonio, you let me worry about that. They know me already in the area and I know most of them. We just need you to act for Mr. Bianchi, with a minimal amount of bloodshed," Tony replied.

"When do you want me to leave Mr. Bianchi?"

"Tony will pick you up tomorrow and you will ride to New York with him."

"Okay, I guess I better head home then and pack."

"Antonio, you have become one of my best guys, and I expect you will do well. But be careful. It seems that I am not the only one interested in this market. There has been word that Giovanni Caprino has his men there, and they are also trying to put the squeeze on the dealers. We have to get to them and make this deal before he does. If they get in the way, you know what to do. Comprende?"

"Yes, sir. It will be taken care of."

"Okay, now you all leave. I am tired and have to rest."

The gentlemen kissed Mr. Bianchi's ring and then left the office. Once outside the office they stopped in the hallway.

"Antonio, I will pick you up around nine."

"I will be ready; just give a blow on the ole horn. Ciao."

***

Later that evening Antonio and Maria were at the dining room table.

"Babe, I need you to pack up a bag for me. I am going to be gone for about a week."

"I know you hate questions, but where to, may I ask?"

"Yes I do, but if you need to know, I am going to New York City on business."

"Bianchi business?"

"No, monkey business. Yes, of course for Mr. Bianchi. You know what? You should really have a little more respect for him. He provides us with everything we have."

"Respect him? He is nothing but a thief and a murderer. He sits in that fine home like a coward making you do all his dirty work. I just worry that one of these days you are going to leave to do his business and never come back."

Antonio got up from his chair, walked up behind Maria, and placed his hands on her shoulders.

"Don't worry, dollface. I won't get into anything I can't get out of…I promise."

"Okay, as long as you promise. Now, go sit down and finish your supper. I will take care of your bag after dessert."

Antonio sat down and went back to his meal.

Chapter Ten
Enter the Drug Wars

The following morning Antonio was drinking his coffee when a horn sounded outside.

"Okay, babe, it's time to go. I will call you when we get settled in at the hotel. I will be at the Luxor Hotel on West 46th Street."

"You just be careful, okay? I love you."

"I promise you I will. I love you too."

Antonio took his jacket and bag and went out the door.

"Yeah, don't get yourself killed, you bastard. I want to see you hang!"

***

After a long couple of days of driving, Antonio and Tony DeStephano sat in the hotel room and discussed their meeting for later that afternoon.

"We are going to meet with this guy named Morris Mclauren at three. He seems to be the head man for the heroin traffic on the south side. He will be heavily guarded, so we don't want to make any quick moves.

This has got to be done with tact. We get him onboard and then help him take over the north side. This way there is only one spook to deal with," Tony said as he sat on the edge of the bed.

"What happens if he doesn't want to play ball?"

"Well, then we get with the man handling the north side. The guy's name is Kim Knott, and if McLauren won't join us, then we get Knott to join. We will then give him the same deal; we help him take over all the New York trade. Once that is done, he will deal directly with us. Either way, Mr. Bianchi will get his cut."

"When it comes to making the deal, Tony, I have an idea to ensure that we get Mr. Bianchi his fifteen percent."

"Okay shoot; what are you planning?"

"We go in there and ask for twenty percent. We will let them get us down to fifteen percent, and then the dumbass Negroes will think they pulled a deal."

"Are you sure you want to play like that? You could actually blow the whole deal that way."

"Hear me out, Tony. Mr. Bianchi put me in this position for a reason. I will get him his cut. Shit, you never know…they might fold on twenty percent, which would really make the boss happy."

***

Later that day a car pulled up beside the abandoned factory where Morris hung out. Antonio and Tony stepped out of the car, and two black men with machine guns approached them; one of them was Joseph Smith, a young man who was nothing but muscle. He motioned for the other man, Antwan Davis, to pat down their visitors. "Check these guys out. Mr. McLauren doesn't want any surprises."

Tony DeStephano spoke up quickly. "We aren't carrying. This is strictly business, my friend."

"First off, asshole, I am not your friend, and this is how we do business."

The other man finished patting them down and shook his head.

"Okay, good. Antonio, follow me."

***

McLauren sat in the middle of the factory with a couple of bodyguards on each side, and a young scantily dressed black woman on his lap. He raised his hand, and the young lady stood and went to stand with one of the body guards.

"Well, well, if it isn't some more white faces from Chicago. Go ahead and have a seat."

Antonio and Tony sat down on the two chairs that were in front of McLauren.

"So, you two want to come to New York City and hone in on my business. One of your types has already been here, and I will give you the same answer I gave him. I don't need you and your bosses to help me. We are doing just fine without you."

"Listen, we aren't here because you need help. Your boys on the street are the ones that really need our help. In exchange for that help you will give Mr. Bianchi a sort of insurance payment."

"I am not paying any guinea any insurance."

Antonio raised his hand. "Hear me out. We already have half the New York City police force on our payroll, along with the mayor and a few others. We can ensure that you have no interference with your dealings."

"Okay, I will hear you out. What will this so-called insurance cost me?"

"Mr. Bianchi will take care of you, and you will give him twenty percent off the top."

"You are out of your mind. The other cracker that came in here trying to strong-arm me only wanted fifteen percent, and I told him to shove it. You two better get out of here before I start getting angry; my boys here don't like seeing me get angry. They get a little trigger happy."

"I don't care what Caprino and his boys came here with. They have no way to protect your investments like we do. We have the manpower and the politicians. So you can work with us...or maybe there is someone else."

"I can tell you this, you son of a bitch. Knott won't work with you either. If he does we will wipe his little nigger ass out, and you along with him."

"How about we offer you this? How about you join up with us, pay Mr. Bianchi his cut, and in return we'll help you take over all of New York City?"

"You're saying that together we will take out the north side?"

"That is what I am saying."

"Now that is an interesting proposal. But I won't give up more than five percent."

"That will not make Mr. Bianchi happy. I tell you what. I will give you twenty-four hours to think about it. The deal is twenty percent, and total control of the heroin market in New York City. After that, the deal is closed. Tony, let's go and give this man some time to think. We will be back tomorrow for your answer." Antonio and Tony got up from their seats and began to walk toward the door.

"Wait...I tell you what. You contact your boss and tell him I'll do twelve percent and not a penny more."

Antonio turned around and faced Morris.

"You have twenty-four hours. Sleep on it."

Antonio turned around, and he and Tony walked out the door. As they walked to their car and got inside, they discussed the situation.

"I think we are going to have to make a trip north. This spook is a real pill."

"I think you're right, Antonio. I will get in touch with Knott and set up a meeting for tomorrow night at the Kit Kat Club. Let him come to us."

***

The following evening inside the club there was a young half-dressed woman on stage dancing on a pole, while other scantily dressed women danced around the club, some on guys' laps. Antonio, Tony, Kim Knott, and Knott's bodyguard Darius Biggs were sitting at a table in the corner as they discussed the offer from Mr. Bianchi.

"Okay, Kim, here is the deal. We tried to offer it to your counterpart on the south side yesterday, and he didn't see the value in what we were offering. I am hopeful that a businessman like you has better insight," said Tony.

"So, Morris was his usual asshole self I gather. Well, I can say one thing, he may have a lot of men and connections, but he has no clue about running a business. What type of deal are you talking?"

"Mr. Knott, we have the manpower, the backing of the police, and the mayor. We want you to join us, and have you control the heroin market here in New York City," replied Antonio.

"Okay, but what's the catch? You son a bitchen' guineas always want something."

Antonio stood up from his seat, and so did Darius. Both men pulled out their pistols and pointed them at each other's faces.

"You better watch your damn language, you no account nigga."

Darius quickly replied. "Mister, if I were you I would sit back down. I have no problem causing a scene, or putting a nice big hole in the pretty shirt of yours."

Antonio held onto his pistol with a very steady hand, waiting to fire. "You don't have to talk like that, okay? We are offering a business deal. This is not some street thug meeting."

"Kim, you need to have your man put away his heater. Antonio, sit down. Let's keep this business-like."

"Darius, sit down, put away your gun, and let's hear this through."

"Yes, sir, Mr. Knott."

Antonio sat back in his chair. Darius was much slower and kept his pistol on the table in plain sight.

112

"Mr. Knott, it is like this. You would control the market, and we get twenty-five percent of everything off the top."

"Damn, that is an awfully big cut," Knott replied.

"That ain't no cut, that's bullshit; bullshit, I tell you. Come on, Mr. Knott, let's get the hell out of here."

"Darius, if you don't shut the hell up you're going back to Nigeria. Got it?"

"Yes, sir. Sorry."

"Okay, now let's get back to business. Mr. Knott, you need to think about what we will be providing. Not only protection for your dealers on the street, but if you run into any trouble, we can use our influence with the mayor and others to get you out of it. All the while you're controlling all the heroin traffic in New York," explained Tony.

"So, you're saying that we will take out McLauren and you provide me some protection. What about your counterpart, that ummm…Mr. Caprino? They talked to me already and wanted to give me a deal. What is to say that they won't take us all out?"

"Caprino and his boys are not a problem. We have more men, and they don't have the mayor. He doesn't want his goons to get into a firefight with us. So what do you think? You ready to take on all of New York City?"

"I still think twenty-five percent is steep. I tell you what, I will do fifteen percent of every Cadillac sold."

"What Cadillac? We are talking drugs here, not cars," Antonio replied.

"Man, this whitey just ain't up to speed. Mister, a Cadillac around here is an ounce of heroin," Darius laughed.

Antonio had begun to get upset with Darius's remarks. "Now you listen...we aren't playing games!" Antonio took in a deep breath. "But I can see that you are businessmen, and need to keep your costs low. I tell you what. I will lower it to twenty percent. That's the deal, and I suggest you take it. Your counterpart will deal if you won't."

Kim rubbed his chin and shook his head in a positive manner. "Twenty percent...okay, done. So, when do we start this thing?"

"We will be in contact with you in a week. This has got to be planned out properly. Don't make any moves until we say to," Tony replied.

"You know it. It will be a pleasure to do business with you and your boss."

Tony lifted his glass of wine as the other three men lifted their drinks, and they all touched them together.

"Gentlemen, a toast to business," Tony said as the glasses touched.

"To business," Knott and the others quickly replied.

"Darius, put that heater away," Knott said as he hit Darius in the shoulder.

"Okay, okay," Darius replied as he put his pistol back into its holster.

Tony took over the conversation from there. "This is what is going to happen. Some of my boys and me will take out McLauren at his warehouse."

Knott broke in. "Where do you want us to be?"

"I don't. This is the thing…we need you and all your guys to be off the street and have very strong alibis. The cops need to think this was done by someone else, not you or your boys. So I don't want any blacks at the hit."

"Hey, man, that's cool with me. I didn't want to screw with McLauren anyway. You and your boys can take care of it."

"Listen, you need to just hear me out. We will take out McLauren at his warehouse, and the finger will be pointed at our friend Caprino. Once things are clear, you can either take in his guys or take them out of the picture and use your own men. That is up to you."

"His guys will listen to me once Morris is dead, and since they know their customers there is no need starting from scratch."

"That sounds good. Once a month I will meet with you and you will give me Mr. Bianchi's percentage."

"I assure you we will work with you without any problems. Isn't that right, Darius?"

"Yes, sir, Mr. Knott."

"Good," Tony said, signaling for the waitress. "Why don't we get a bite to eat, then hit the town?"

"Sounds good to me…I'm starved," replied Darius.

The four gentlemen continued to talk as they watched the girls dancing and had a few drinks.

***

The next morning Antonio was in his hotel room packing to head back to Chicago. As he packed, there was a knock on the door.

"I'll be right with you." Antonio picked up his .45 caliber pistol from the dresser before approaching the door. He looked through the peephole and saw that it was Tony DeStephano, so he laid the pistol on the table beside the door before opening the door.

"Good morning."

"Yeah, good morning. Are you getting ready to head back to Chicago?"

"Yeah, the wife gets wired when I have been gone too long."

"I know how that can be. That's why I will never get married. Anyway, tell Mr. Bianchi that everything is all set. We will take out Morris and his boys in a few days and the territory will go to Knott. We will keep a close eye on his operations to make sure that he gets his proper cut."

"What about Caprino? How are you going to keep him off their backs?"

"Oh, don't worry. I have a little surprise brewing for Caprino's boys. Let's just say that they are going to be a bit tied up with the fuzz."

"That really sounds good to me. But I need to get going. I'm flying back at noon and don't want to miss my flight. Good luck with Knott and the rest of them."

"Grazie. Come out to New York anytime you want, and bring the missus. I am sure she would love to take in a show and do some shopping. Oh, and by the way, Antonio…I am really impressed with how you worked this deal. You are going places."

"Thanks, Tony. I think that bringing the wife here and letting her loose shopping in New York City would scare me more than Caprino any day."

"I know what you mean. Dames can be dangerous in a store with a bunch of green. You have a safe trip back to Chicago."

"Thanks. I'll be talking to ya soon."

Tony turned around and headed out the door as Antonio closed the door and returned to his packing.

***

A few days later, Maria was in the living room when the phone rang.

"Hello, Capresi residence."

"Hey, Maria, this is Gianna."

"Hey, what is going on?"

"We need to get together with Johnny and Danny. They have some info put together—a lot of information—and need to get it to you."

"Oh really! That is great. Let's see. Antonio leaves the house around nine, and I don't want to chance him coming home for lunch. Can you all come over like ten?"

"Yeah, and Danny suggested that we should arrive separately. I will be there first."

"That sounds good to me. Talk to you then."

Maria hung up the phone.

"I bet this is going to be good!"

***

At 9:55 the next morning there was a knock at the door, and Maria opened it to find Gianna.

"Hey, Maria. The others will be along in a few minutes."

"That's fine. Would you like some coffee?"

"I would love some."

"I have some cookies that I made also. Let me get the coffee going and I will be right in."

Just as Maria walked into the kitchen, another knock sounded at the door.

"Hey, Gianna, could you get that for me?"

"Sure, not a problem."

Gianna got up from the couch and walked over to the door.

"Who is it?"

"Open the door, sis. It's me and Danny."

Gianna opened the door and the two men walked inside.

"Hi, Johnny. Hi, Danny. Would you two like some coffee?" Maria yelled from the kitchen.

"Sure," both men replied.

"Okay, you two, go ahead and have a seat in the living room and I will be right in."

Moments later Maria walked in with coffee and cookies for her guests.

"Well, I must say that I am glad to see you two. I am sure you have a bunch of dirt on my good-for-nothing husband."

"Yeah, we have a bunch of info to give you on what Antonio has been up to these past couple of weeks," Johnny replied.

"I hope you take this okay. I hate to be the bearer of this kind of crap." Danny looked concerned about the information he had to give her.

"She will be fine. She knows how he is, and has suspected all this stuff for a long time. Just lay it out to her."

Maria set the coffee and cookies on the table.

"Danny believe me, I know what I am dealing with. What kind of dirt do you have on that no-account loser of a husband?"

Danny reached into his attaché case and pulled out a folder filled with pictures and notes. He opened the folder and spread out all the pictures. Maria started to rummage through them and picked up the one of Antonio as he kissed Sarah Johnson outside the apartment in West Chicago.

"Now, Maria, please don't blow your wig. But, as you can see, he has himself a moll. In fact, he has picked up a couple of women in the Eldorado Club and brought them to an apartment on the west side. But this one here, a Miss Sarah Johnson, has been with him for a couple of weeks now."

"Oh, I figured he had another dame, but I didn't know he had an actual apartment…that little son of a bitch. No wonder he would come home late and look like he just walked out of the bedroom ready to leave for the day."

"I am so sorry, Maria. But I have to give you what I find."

"No, you're doing a great job, Danny. I really appreciate it."

Maria wiped a tear that had rolled down her cheek. "What else do you have?"

"Well, do you remember about a week and a half ago when Mr. Colombo's Hardware was robbed and he was snuffed?"

"Yeah, I remember hearing that. It was a shame they killed him. My dad worked for him long ago."

Danny pulled out pictures of Antonio as he ran out of the store with his gun in his hand.

"Well, seems that it wasn't a robbery at all. Mr. Bianchi put a hit out on Colombo for some reason, and Antonio was the cooler."

"Oh my god! He didn't kill another one. I am sure he is the one that shot Caprino's son, Stephano, and now Mr. Colombo too?"

"Yeah, sorry. I liked Mr. Colombo too. Okay, now this little trip he just took. Seems he headed to New York City and was doing some type of business with a couple of the blacks there. So I had a friend look out for him, and the best I can figure is that they are trying to break into the heroin market."

"Now wait a minute...you're telling me first that he killed Mr. Colombo, and that they're getting into drugs now?"

"I hate to throw you that curve, but it appears that way. My friend didn't get any pictures, but he is quite reliable. He said they met with two different blacks known for drug trafficking. Big time dealers, so I am pretty sure they are getting into it pretty deep."

"I just can't believe it...but then again, they never surprise me. Well, it just piles up deeper and deeper.

One day soon I am going to put them all away for a long, long time. I really appreciate all your hard work, Danny."

"Maria, tell you what. I'm not on any other cases right now, so I will keep an eye on him."

"But, Danny, I can't afford to pay you anything. Antonio gives me just enough to get food and stuff."

"Don't worry about it. I hate the mob, and I will do anything in my power to make sure they go down. This guy just keeps me wanting to do more."

"Oh, Danny, I really appreciate it. I will make it up to you some day."

"Don't worry your sweet little head about it. I will keep an eye on this joker. Just promise me that you will be careful, and that you'll put them away for a long time."

"You got it, Danny."

"Good. Hey, I need to run. You better put all that stuff up really good so he doesn't find it."

"Thanks again, Danny. I have a special place he will never find."

"Okay, I will call Gianna whenever I get anything else."

Danny and Maria got up from their seats and Maria walked Danny to the door. Maria gave him a hug and a peck on his cheek.

"I will never forget you, Danny."

"Have a good one, and God bless."

Maria went back to the living room.

"I better take all this and put it away."

She bent over, scooped up all the pictures and notes, and brought them to the bedroom to put in her safe hiding place. She then went back to the living room to chat with Gianna and Johnny. When she got there, Johnny had already put on his jacket.

"Hey, Maria, I need to head out too. I have a good possibility of a job at the wharf. It's a nice paying job and with the union too, plus I need the health insurance for the wife with the baby coming."

"Well, good luck. Let me know how it goes."

"I will. See you later, sis. I will let myself out."

"So, Maria, you okay with all this?"

"I am fine. I knew about the dames, but the killing and the drugs are what really have me floored."

"They have me befuddled too. They didn't tell me about any of this stuff before we came. I am really scared for you now."

"Don't worry. I have everything very well hidden. He has no clue what is coming at him. But when all this shit hits him, he is a dead man."

"Still, you need to watch out. He gets really mad at you one night and he may do something."

"I don't think he would unless Bianchi told him to. He is so far up that man's ass he can't breathe on his own."

***

At the same time, in New York City, three black cars were parked just a block from the factory that McLauren used as his headquarters. Tony DeStephano and Luciano De Luca stood together discussing the hit they were about to make.

"Okay, Luciano, here is the plan. Joey will take his boys around the back side as we drive by and ice the guards out front. Once done, we will turn around, and Giovanni in the back car will drive up and start firing. As soon as Joey hears that, they will go in behind and we will go in front with Giovanni, and get all them niggers in a crossfire. They won't know what hit them. We take out everyone that is in the factory. I want to be certain, though, that McLauren gets plugged. He is the key to this whole thing."

"You're the boss. The boys are ready and waiting on your signal."

"Good. Let's get this over with."

The men got into their cars and all three started down the road. One car turned off between the factories and the other two continued until they reached McLauren's headquarters. Fausto stuck his machine gun out the window and fired on the four men standing in front of the factory doorway, killing them instantly.

Inside the factory, McLauren could be heard yelling, "We're being hit. Get those sons-a-bitches!" Machine gun fire began to pelt the front door area from the inside, but McLauren's men had no clue that at that moment their four other guards were being killed at the back door.

Out in front the second car stopped, and two more men got out and started firing into the thin walls of the warehouse. But the gunfire that was coming from McLauren's men inside the factory forced Tony's men to get behind their cars for protection as they fired.

Meanwhile, Joey and his team made it into the back of the warehouse, and began to kill McLauren's six men that were firing toward the front. Morris McLauren got inside his car and tried to escape through a closed door. He managed to break through the door to the front of the building, but encountered a barrage of gunfire. His tires got blown out first, and Tony's men kept firing until they were sure McLauren was dead.

Tony yelled, "Okay, guys, stop firing. McLauren is dead. Get anyone else that is inside and bring them out front."

Joey Petriani and Jack Palmero emerged a few minutes later with the last two of McLauren's gang.

"Jack, put them against the wall," Tony ordered.

"You heard the man, get up against the wall."

The two men stepped back to the wall.

"Jack, Joey…come here."

Palermo and Petriani quickly did as they were ordered.

"Okay, now plug these guys. We don't need any loose ends." Before the two men could scream, Joey and Jack fired their machine guns at them until they both fell to the ground.

"Okay, Luciano, Fausto, we need to get out of here and set up our alibis. Jack and Joey, I want you guys to head to Jersey for a few days before you go back to Chicago. Just stay out of sight for a while," Tony ordered. "I am going to the house to make a special phone call."

Tony got into his car and drove straight to his home. Once there he went inside and called the cops.

Within moments the police dispatcher was on the other end.

"Hello, police?"

"Yes, this is dispatch. What can I do for you, sir?"

"It's what I can do for you. It seems that the blacks that do the heroin stuff down at the warehouses have been attacked."

"How do you know that?"

"I heard a couple of guys talking at the club a minute ago. They said they hit some guy named McLauren."

"Is that a fact? What is your name, sir?"

"I would rather not say, but the guys were mobsters that work for that guy Joey Esposito, who is Mr. Caprino's New York underboss."

Tony then hung up the phone and walked into his kitchen, laughing.

***

Within minutes the police dispatcher sent a couple of cars to Joey Esposito's office in downtown New York City. They went up the elevator and walked right past Esposito's secretary. The first to greet Mr. Esposito was Detective Danny LeRoux.

"Well, well, well, Mr. Joseph Esposito. We need to stop meeting like this."

"LeRoux, what the hell do you want?"

"Well, seems like we got a call that you put a hit on someone, and I want you to take a little ride downtown so that we can talk about it."

"I didn't hit anyone. I have been here in my office all day. Just ask my secretary."

"I am sure that she would alibi for you. I assure you we will pull your phone records also. Come with us the easy way. You know the routine."

"This has got to be that Bianchi son of a bitch. I bet his boys were involved. Okay, let's go do this so I can get back to work."

Joey got up from behind his desk and LeRoux cuffed him and walked him out of the office.

Joey yelled out to his secretary. "Call my attorney and have him meet me downtown."

"Yes, Mr. Esposito," she replied as she picked up the phone.

***

Three days later Tony and Luciano were in the Kit Kat Club having lunch.

"Okay, now that McLauren is out of the way we have another spook to fill with some daylight," Tony said nonchalantly.

"What? I thought we were going to use him to run the show while we just take a cut."

"Are you out of your mind? You actually think a Sicilian like Mr. Bianchi is going to let some jiggaboo run part of his business? No way! The whole meeting with Knott was to get his confidence and to give us time to take McLauren out. Now we finish up business and take over the heroin market ourselves. We need to find Knott's operation and then set up a meeting. This is what Mr. Bianchi wanted all along. Get your men to find him and I will take care of the rest."

"Okay, Tony. If that is what Mr. Bianchi wants."

"Luciano, go ahead and promote one of the guys to be over just the heroin stuff. Who do you think could handle it?"

"Well, boss, I think that it should be Fausto. He is smart with numbers and not a man to mess with. But at the same time he is cool-headed enough to work with the cops and the mayor."

"Okay, make him capo over the drugs. As far as Knott goes, I want you to contact him. Make a meeting with him at his house on Tuesday night. That way we will be sure that he is home. I will get some of the boys together, and then we will hit him so hard his family in Africa will feel it."

"You have it, boss. I will let you know when it is set."

"Good. Now let's just enjoy these babes."

Tony and Luciano sat and drank and watched the dancers.

G. R. Holton & Marlene Mendoza

Chapter Eleven
Go West Young Man

In Chicago Mr. Bianchi and Antonio were in the library of Mr. Bianchi's home, smoking cigars and talking about business.

"Antonio, I have asked you here to speak with you privately. I talked to Tony, and he told me about how you handled things in New York City. You have become quite the businessman. I asked for fifteen percent, and you walked away with them giving me twenty. I am quite impressed to say the least."

Antonio replied with a sideways grin. "I learned it all from you, sir."

"Well, that makes me feel good. You have learned well. I have a major business proposition, which could prove very lucrative for you and your family. I have acquired two casinos in Las Vegas, and I need someone to run the business out there for me. You will have all the men you need, and the financing to get started. Now, I know you don't have a casino background, but from what I have seen, it will not take you long to learn."

"You know I would do anything you ask, but Maria has lived here all her life with her family. It may take me a bit to convince her to move west."

"Antonio, I need you out there. I am sure you will be able to convince her. I tell you what…why don't you take a couple of days off? Take Maria for a trip, just the two of you…an elegant cruise or something. I will take care of everything. That way the two of you can talk, and it will be easier to convince her of what is the right thing to do. You will no longer be just a capo, Antonio…you will be my Las Vegas underboss, in control of the whole thing. No more being a street thug. You will live a life of luxury. You and Maria could have anything you want. Penthouse apartment, nice clothes for Maria from the best shops, fancy car…the whole ball of wax. Comprende?"

"Yes, Mr. Bianchi, I fully understand. I think I will take you up on the trip. Let me talk to Maria. It's going to take me a bit to convince her, but I know I can get her to go."

"Very good. You let me know. I will make you a very happy, rich man, Antonio."

"Grazie, Mr. Bianchi. I will see you as soon as I get back."

"I am glad. When you are going out, find Jackie. Tell him I said to give you five-thousand dollars. That should be more than enough to have a good time."

"Thanks, Mr. Bianchi. That is quite generous of you."

Antonio got out of his seat, kissed Bianchi's ring, and then walked out of the library. He then walked down the hallway to where Jackie and Tony DeStephano were in the middle of a game of billiards.

"Hey, Jackie, as soon as you're finished I need some money, per Mr. Bianchi."

Jackie set down his cue stick. "I can get that for you now...this game may take a bit. How much do you need?"

"He said to get five thousand."

"What are you going to do, buy a house?"

"That's between Mr. Bianchi and me. I don't know if he wants anyone else to know just yet."

"Antonio, I am his consigliere. I know everything going on. I know he wants you in Las Vegas. But anyway, let me go get that for you. It's my shot...I am stripes. Take my turn for me. I will be right back."

Jackie walked away and Antonio picked up the cue stick and took a shot.

"So, Antonio, I guess you are going to be the man in Las Vegas. Nice position," DeStephano said as he took his shot.

"Yeah, Tony, only if I can convince Maria."

"Well, you could always slap her around if she won't. It works for me."

"No, the last time I smacked her she threatened to cut off my manhood. So that is not a choice I will mess with." Antonio looked up as Jackie walked back into the room.

"Here you go, Antonio. Is this a loan or a bonus? I have to make it right in the books."

"It is a bonus I would say, because I didn't ask for it."

"That's good. I will get with our accountant and cover it. You do whatever you have been asked to do, because it would not make Mr. Bianchi happy if you turn him down."

"I promised him I would do my best. You guys have a great day. I need to go start setting things in motion."

Both Jackie and Tony replied. "See ya."

Antonio walked out of the game room and headed home.

***

Late that night Maria and Antonio were in the dining room drinking coffee and eating their dessert.

"Maria, I had a long talk with Mr. Bianchi, and he has made provisions for us to get away for a little trip."

"What have you done now?"

Antonio laughed. "Oh, Maria, you are always the suspicious type. I did nothing at all. He is just showing his appreciation for the work I did in New York City. You and I have tickets on a luxury cruise liner to the Bahamas this coming weekend."

"Really, Antonio? So there is no mob stuff, no meetings on the ship? Just you, me, and the open ocean?"

"Yes, we fly out to New York and catch the ship on Friday. Bring your best dresses…no, wait." Antonio reached into his wallet and pulled out a thousand dollar bill. "Here, take this and go to the best dress and shoe shops downtown. I want you to buy yourself a ballroom

132

dress and shoes. While you're at it, get a couple of outfits for the trip. Anything you need. I want my gal to be the smoothest thing on the ocean."

"Antonio, this is way too much. I wouldn't have a clue what to buy."

"I am sure you can figure it out. Now, I need to go out for a little while, but I won't be late."

Antonio got up and kissed Maria on the cheek, grabbing his jacket off the hook as he went out the door.

"Well, at least I get something out of all this crap. I might as well use it."

Maria picked up the phone and called Theresa. The phone rang a couple of times and Theresa picked up.

"Hello."

"Hey, sis. You are not going to believe this, but Antonio just gave me a thousand dollar bill."

"You have got to be kidding! Okay, what's the deal?"

"I am not sure what he wants, but he said to go dress shopping. I have to keep playing the role of his little wife, so I have to do it. You want to join me?"

"Spending someone else's money is something I do best. I'm in. Where do you want to meet?"

"Let's start with lunch at Babe's at noon, and then we'll hit the stores."

"That sounds good to me, sis. I will just come to your place around eleven thirty, okay?"

"Okay, I'll see you then. Ciao."

"Ciao, sis."

***

The next morning at eleven-thirty there was a knock upon Maria's front door. Maria walked from the kitchen and opened the door to let her sister in.

"Hey, kiddo, you ready to go spend some mob money?" Maria laughed.

"You know it. I have just checked out the phone directory and there are a couple of really good stores to go to."

"Well, we will take a cab to each one and see what they have. But first, I am starving, so let's go to the Lamp Lighter instead. They have great sandwiches there."

"It's your money. I am yours for the day."

"Well I have to be back by five o'clock to fix supper, so we better get a move on it."

Maria grabbed her jacket from behind the door and put it on.

"Okay, let's go."

The two ladies walked out the door and headed for lunch.

***

At eight o'clock on Friday night, Maria and Antonio stood on the bow of the ship with drinks in their hands. Maria was in a long flowing red sequined dress and Antonio was in a black pin-striped suit and tie.

"Hey, Maria, how about you and me go down to the casino and have some fun?"

"You want to go to the casino? I have never played cards and you know it."

"Maybe you will have beginner's luck."

"Okay, I will try...it might just be fun."

Maria was astonished by the elegance and the sheer number of games at the casino.

"Wow, look at this place! How do you know what ones to go to? There are so many tables."

"Well, let's just start at the easiest one first."

"What one would that be, Mr. Gambling Man?" Maria said, laughing.

"Well, ma'am, the easiest to learn is the roulette table. We will start there and work up from that."

"What do you do? Roulette sounds like a French game."

"Well, aren't you the smart one? It is actually from eighteenth century France. Just follow my lead and I will teach you."

The two approached the croupier at the roulette table. "Sir, I would like five hundred in chips. Make them twenties."

"Sure thing, mister."

The spinner counted out the chips and pushed them over to Antonio. Antonio turned to Maria and gave her one hundred in chips.

"Okay, mister gambler, go ahead and teach me."

"We will start simple. Take one chip and select black or red."

"Okay, one chip on black."

Maria took a chip and placed it on the black space and Antonio pulled a chip from his pile.

"Well, I think I am going to play some odds."

Antonio placed his chip at the bottom of the middle row. The operator let the ball go and it went around until it stopped on twenty black. Maria jumped up and down with excitement.

"Hey, it landed on black! I win!"

"What do you know? I won also! But I get more money because of the odds."

"Odds smodds...I won! Okay, let me try again. Can I do more than one?"

"You can do as many as you want, babe. Just remember, the more you put out there, the more you can lose if your number doesn't hit."

"Okay, let's see. I will put one on the zero and another one on the ten."

"Why those?"

"Well...I like zero, and ten was how old I was when I lost my dad."

"I will let mine ride."

"What do you mean by letting it ride?"

"Just means I will leave all of mine where they are."

"Okay."

The croupier let the ball go and it went around until it landed on the ten.

"Wow, talk about beginner's luck. Nice haul, baby."

The operator gave Maria her winnings.

"Oh my gosh...I won all of that?"

"Yeah, seven hundred dollars. The odds are thirty-five to one on each number."

"I could get use to this."

"Are you ready to move on to something harder?"

"Can I just stay here for a little longer?"

"Maria, dear, you can do whatever you want. We are here to have fun."

"Okay, let's see. I think I will do thirty-five, thirty-two, and zero again."

"I think I will watch you this time."

The croupier again let the ball go and it went around until it landed on the zero.

Antonio jumped up. "Damn, girl…you seem to be good at this."

The croupier gave Maria her winnings.

"Yeah, I like this."

"Cool…let 'em ride?"

"No, I am changing my numbers. Twenty and five."

The croupier let the ball go, and it landed on thirty-two.

"Oh man…you should have listened," Antonio said with a laugh.

"Okay, funny guy. Can you go get me a drink?"

"Sure, what do you want?"

"I just want a nice glass of burgundy."

"Okay, I'll be right back. Don't lose all your chips."

"Oh, I will try not to."

Antonio walked away and Maria continued to play.

***

In New York City Tony DeStephano and Luciano De Luca were in a hotel room cleaning their machine guns.

"Okay, let's get this right so no one gets hurt. I need you to take Jack, and I will take Vinny, and we will drive to Knott's house. I want to spray the place and take out anyone that is inside," Tony said.

"I think we should go in afterwards and check to make sure that every spook inside is dead, especially Knott and Biggs, because they can finger us."

"Tell you what. You take both Jack and Vinny and clear the house. Take their weapons, too. We don't want some street dealer thinking that if they have weapons that they were taking over. This is the end of these damn spooks."

"You got it, boss."

***

Later that evening the two cars pulled up outside of Kim Knott's house and parked. The darkness and the fact that the men were all dressed in dark suits with ski masks made them virtually invisible. They got out of the vehicles and immediately began to open fire on the house.

Seconds later someone from inside began to return fire. The men all got behind the cars as the gunplay continued. One man ran out the door firing his weapon and was riddled with bullets until he fell over the rail.

"Okay, Luciano, take the boys and go clean house. I will meet you back at the hotel. We need to establish our alibi."

"Will do boss. Jack, Vinny, you heard the man. Let's go take 'em out."

"Head over to my room after this is done. I have a phone call to make."

Tony got back into his car and drove away. He went to his room at the hotel and waited for a half an hour before he picked up the phone to call police dispatch.

"Hello, this is the police. How may I help you?"

"I have some information on a shooting that happened earlier."

"What is your name, sir?"

"I prefer to stay anonymous because the mob is involved, and I know there are leaks in your force."

"What information do you have then?"

"It was a mob hit, and the guys that shot those poor blacks were from Giovanni Caprino's gang. It was Joseph Esposito and two other guys."

"Are you positive?"

"I saw them there with my own two eyes. They got out of a long black car and began shooting up the place."

"Are you sure you can't give me your name or come down and file a report?"

Tony hung up the telephone and laughed.

"That should keep Caprino's boys busy for a little bit."

***

Several hours later four police squad cars pulled up in front of Joseph Esposito's home. A long black car pulled up with them, and police detective Danny LeRoux got out. LeRoux walked to the door and began to bang on it.

"Esposito, this is the police. Open the door with your hands up."

Moments later Joseph opened the door.

"Well, Joseph Esposito, we meet again. This is almost becoming a career for me."

"Oh no, LeRoux. Can't you see it is almost three o'clock in the morning?"

"I can see that, but I need you to come down to headquarters and answer a few questions."

"Why should I?"

"First, because you're such a nice guy, and second, because I have a warrant. The third—and I saved the best for last—you can come quietly or I will physically assist you. It's up to you."

"Can I at least get dressed?"

"Yeah, I guess. One of the officers will go upstairs with you. I just don't want any funny business."

"Yeah, whatever. I'm innocent. I don't care what you flatfoots want. I have been home all night."

"We'll see."

Joseph turned and headed up the stairs to his bedroom, followed by two police officers.

***

Antonio and Maria had moved to the blackjack table.

"Are you having fun, babe?" Antonio asked Maria.

"Yes, believe it or not, I am having a blast. Winning all this money surely helps too."

"Yes, you have done pretty well for yourself. I do have something I need to talk to you about though."

"What's that?"

"Well, Mr. Bianchi has purchased a couple of casinos in Las Vegas and is working a deal on a couple more."

"You said that this was a vacation and had nothing to do with your work."

"I know what I said. But this is important."

"Okay, so what does that have to do with us? "

"You know how you are always saying that you want me off the street?"

"Yeah."

"Well, he wants me to manage the casinos for him."

"You mean move all the way out to Nevada? Are you are asking me to leave Chicago?"

"Yeah. We would have our own home, a nice car, and the clothes that you really deserve."

"But, Antonio, you know all my family is in Chicago. I have lived there all my life. How could you even think of asking me to leave them?"

Maria got up from the table, crying as she ran away. Antonio picked up their chips and dropped a few on the table for the dealer.

"Damn, women...keep the cards hot, Charlie. I'll be back."

Within moments he reached their cabin and walked in. He found Maria lying across the bed crying.

"Maria...dollface...stop crying. Let me explain this. Mr. Bianchi is offering me a great opportunity. There will be no more street hits. Everything is legit. Mr. Bianchi wants me to manage the casinos for him, and in exchange we will be able to buy the house you've always wanted, and maybe even start a family."

"You know how close I am to my mom and sister. I don't think I could just up and move away like that, especially for anything that has to do with the mob."

"Listen to me. You could have the best things, and fly back to visit your family anytime you wanted."

"I don't know, Antonio. This is way too sudden for me to even think of an answer."

"I know this is sudden. Maybe in a year or so you could move them out to Henderson and they would be close."

"You mean pull them up from their roots too? You are just so self-centered, I swear. It's all about Mr. Bianchi and what your needs are."

"Please listen to me, babe. I know I dropped this on you. We have four more days on this cruise. Let's have a good time, and you can think about it."

"What about the other gangsters? They are already out there. Don't you think there will still be trouble?"

"Maria, the greatest thing about this chance is that everyone out there is keeping things legal like, so we don't have to worry. Now, go fix your makeup, and let's go get a bite to eat and a nice bottle of wine. Then we will go dancing. I know you like dancing. What do you say?"

"Well, okay. Give me a few minutes to straighten up and I will meet you back at the blackjack table."

"That's my girl. See you in a little bit."

Antonio walked out of the room and headed back to the casino. Maria then got up from the bed, walked into the bathroom, and began to fix her makeup.

"I can't believe that bastard wants to take me away from my family. But I have to do it if I'm ever going to put his ass away. I sure hope Momma understands. It will only be for a couple of months, then I will drop the bomb on him and return to Chicago."

Chapter Twelve
Welcome To Sin City

A week had passed and Antonio and Maria had returned from their cruise. Antonio was dressed and stood up from the kitchen table after breakfast.

"Maria, I need to get going. I have to meet with Mr. Bianchi this morning. I have to give him the answer today."

"I know, babe. I am still uneasy about moving, but if you feel it will make a better life for us and a chance for a real family, then we will have to go."

"I think it is best. I will more than likely be late tonight, so don't wait up."

"Okay, I will see you later. Love you."

"Love you too."

Antonio grabbed his coat and walked out the door.

"I hate you, Antonio. I will be so happy when you're gone!"

***

A few more hours passed and Mr. Bianchi and Antonio were in the library discussing Antonio's future.

"I hope you had a good time on your cruise."

"Yes, sir. The cruise went better than I expected. At first Maria was very torn up about the whole moving idea. But after talking with her, I was able to convince her that it would be best for us."

"Okay…so you are going to take over my casinos and be my underboss in Nevada. That not only goes for Las Vegas, Antonio, but for Reno also. I am looking to expand the business up there. I am expecting a lot from you."

"You know I will do my very best, Mr. Bianchi."

"I know, Antonio, you always have. Let's talk money. You will get ten percent of everything that comes into the casinos. Twenty-five percent comes back here to me. The rest of the profits are to go to expanding our empire in Nevada. That will include a ten percent split with Mr. Greco in Reno to get a parcel of land to build two brand new casinos in the southern region of Reno. Comprende?"

"I fully understand, and I think that is most generous of you."

"Believe me, Antonio, you will earn every penny. When can you get out there and get to work?"

"Well, I need to get the apartment packed up and shipped. I would say two weeks tops."

"Two weeks is good. Get your family ready and get things done, as I need you out there as soon as possible."

"I won't let you down, Mr. Bianchi. I guarantee you that."

"Oh, and I need you to understand one last thing. I want reports every month, and if I ever find that you're screwing me...well, let's just say you wouldn't want anything to happen to your family. Capiche?"

"Yes, sir. You have no worries there."

Antonio kissed Bianchi's ring, then turned and left the library.

***

Later that afternoon, Maria, Theresa, and Brigitta were all at the kitchen table in Brigitta's apartment, having some tea.

"It is so nice to have my girls here for tea. It has been a while."

"Well, Momma, there is a reason I have asked you and Theresa to have tea with me this afternoon."

"There is? Are you pregnant?"

"No, Momma, I am not pregnant. I wish it was that simple."

"Oh, I was hoping you were going to tell me that I was going to be a grandmother."

"No, I am sorry, but...Antonio and I have to move."

"What do you mean move? Are you getting a house?"

"Well, sort of. We are moving to Nevada."

"What? Nevada? Why?"

Theresa jumped up from her chair. "What the hell are you talking about?"

"Theresa, you need to watch your mouth. I didn't bring you up to talk like that."

"I'm sorry, Momma, but we are moving to Nevada so that Antonio can take over Mr. Bianchi's casinos. He is taking him off the streets and making him a manager."

"A manager? No...he is not going to be a manager; he is being made his underboss. That is no different than what he is doing, other than he will have other people do his killing for him. You will be so far away."

"I know, Momma, and I wish I could change it, but I am going to put him away. I can't do it if he is in Nevada without me. I promise that I will come back regularly."

"Are you sure about this, Maria?" Theresa asked. "It could be quite dangerous out there."

"How much more dangerous could it be compared to what I have been doing here for the past few years?"

Theresa paced back and forth. "Very! You won't have any help! You would be on your own!"

"I know what I am doing. I promised Papa that I would take Antonio out for what he did, and I am not about to give up now."

Brigitta cried. "I don't know, Maria. I agree with your sister. You don't know what is out there. Maybe it is time to give up on your promise and leave Antonio."

"No, Momma...there is no way I am quitting now. He is the man that took my father away, and I am going to be the one to pay him back."

"I don't trust that snake, but I understand that you have to finish what you started. Please be very careful, and make sure you call me every day," Theresa pleaded.

"You want me to call every day, Theresa? How about once a week? Just kidding. I will call you so much it will feel like I am living with you."

"Oh, baby. Please, if you run into any trouble you're to come home right away," Brigitta cried.

"I will, Momma."

"I am going to be so worried about you."

"I know, Momma. Let's change the subject before we all start crying."

"Well, I am not done yet. When are you leaving?"

"We have already begun to get packed, and have to be in Nevada in a week and a half."

"So soon?"

"Yes, Momma. But I will come by before we go."

"How about I come over and give you a hand?" Theresa said as she sat back down.

"That would be great, sis."

"I will come over too. We can get it done a lot quicker if the three of us work together, and I won't be just sitting here worrying about you."

"Oh, thank you, Momma. I really love the both of you, and appreciate it."

***

Later that evening Antonio came in and hung up his jacket. Maria was in the living room listening to the radio.

"I thought you were going to be late?"

"Yeah, I just needed to come home to get some stuff ready. I am going to fly out to Vegas for a couple of days so that I can secure an apartment for us until we find the house you want. In addition to that, Mr. Bianchi wants me to take a look at the casinos."

"How many days do you need to be packed for?"

"I would say three. I will then come back and help you pack the rest of the things."

"Oh, I met with my mom and Theresa, and they are going to come and help pack."

"How did they take the move idea?"

"They were just as upset as I was when you first told me. Momma was really mad."

"Babe, like I said, in a few months, once we get set in a home, you can come back to visit. I will start making a lot of big money, and we will bring her out to Nevada so she is close to you again."

"I know, Antonio. I am just going to miss them so badly."

"I fully understand, babe. Is there anything to eat? I'm hungry."

"Yeah, go sit down and I will whip something together for you. Do you want some coffee too?"

"Yeah, that would be great."

Maria got up to prepare dinner for Antonio.

***

The following morning Maria got up early and packed Antonio's suitcase for him. Within minutes, Antonio woke and went in to take his shower to get ready. Just as she finished, Antonio came out of the bathroom.

"Everything all set, babe?" Antonio asked.

"Yeah, you are all set up."

"Excuse me?" he replied.

"I meant you are all set up to go on your trip."

"Oh…the way you talk sometimes. Weird. Anyway, so I have enough for a couple of days?"

"Yeah, you're good to go for at least three days."

"Thank you. You're a doll!"

Antonio took a suit out of the closet and got dressed.

***

Three days passed and Antonio returned from Nevada. It was a regular day like any other. Antonio ate his breakfast and headed out to work. Maria went into the bedroom and began to unpack Antonio's suitcase so she could wash the clothes he had used. In the middle of the chore, she found a pair of ladies' panties tucked inside a side compartment of the suitcase.

"That no good, son-of-a-bitch husband of mine! He went out there to set something up all right. He wanted to make sure he has a moll lined up for when we move there. I swear, I could kill him myself; but then I wouldn't be any better than him. I'd better put these back so he won't know I found them. I don't want to get into it with him. That would screw up everything."

Maria finished with the rest of the clothes, then stuffed the panties back into the suitcase where she'd found them. When she finished, she went to the bathroom and washed her hands in disgust.

***

One week later, Maria and Theresa were busy packing.

"Theresa, I need you to do me a really big favor."

"What, sis?"

"I need you to take the book and pictures, and hold on to them for me until I need them. I can't chance Antonio finding them while we unpack. Once we get settled and I know his routine, I will have you send them to me."

"I can do that. I don't think anything will happen."

"Great! Let me go get it, and you can just put it in your purse so it is not out in the open."

Maria went into her bedroom and returned moments later with a notebook and a stack of pictures.

"Here you go. Make sure you put them away. If anything ever happens to me, I want you to take them to the judge. I don't think that he is on the payroll, and he will be able to take down Bianchi and Antonio at least."

Maria placed everything into an envelope and handed it to Theresa. Theresa then took the envelope and placed it into her purse.

"Not a problem, sis. One way or another, these assholes are going to go down. You just be careful out there, okay?"

"No problem. Plus, I will come home a few times a year."

Maria and Theresa hugged, tears rolling down their cheeks. Suddenly, there was a knock at the door and Maria walked over to answer it.

"Who is it?"

"It is Brigitta."

Maria opened the door to let her mother in.

"So, today is the big day," Brigitta said as Maria took her jacket.

"Yes, Momma. The movers will be here anytime now, and once everything is packed in the truck I will be heading to the airport. Antonio is already in Las Vegas."

"Well, I made some cookies for your flight." Brigitta handed Maria a paper sack.

"Awww, thank you Momma."

"Just remember, if you have any trouble at all I want you to come home right away."

"I will. Believe me, if anything at all happens I will get out of there right away."

Maria and Brigitta hugged each other fiercely as tears flowed down both of their cheeks.

"I am sorry, baby, I can't stay for this. It is making me way too sad."

"I understand, Momma. I promise I will be fine, and I will be back in a couple of months."

Maria walked her mother to the door and found the movers on their way up the stairway.

"Looks like your movers are here. Be careful, and call me as soon as you get into Las Vegas. Please stay out of trouble!"

"I will try, Momma. Love you."

"I love you too."

Brigitta turned from the doorway and pulled her rosary from under her jacket. "Please, dear Mother Mary, protect my daughter."

Brigitta continued down the stairway as the men walked up to the door.

G. R. Holton & Marlene Mendoza

Chapter Thirteen
Home Sweet Vegas Home

Two months passed, and it was a beautiful day in Nevada. Antonio had bought a house on the outskirts of Las Vegas and they were pretty well settled in. Maria and Antonio were in their new living room relaxing on a Saturday afternoon.

"Antonio, I must say this house is great…much more than I could have ever dreamed of."

"Babe, this is just the beginning. The more casinos that Mr. Bianchi opens will mean the more money I will be making, and I will give you everything you deserve."

"And in return I will give you everything you deserve."

"There you go talking weird again. What do you mean by that?"

"Oh silly, you are on the defensive today. I mean a family, and a wife you will be proud of."

"I am already proud of you. As far as the family, let's hold that thought for a little while until I really get things going."

"You may be just a little late for that."

"Huh?"

"You know, for such a smart businessman, you don't take a hint too well, do you?"

"What are you talking about?"

"I guess I have to spell it out for you. You're going to be a father."

"Oh my God! You're pregnant?"

"I think that is what you being a father means."

"I am not sure what to say. You need to take it easy now. I don't want you to lift a finger around here. I will get you a maid. Yeah, that's what I will do, get a maid."

"Whoa…slow down there, cowboy! I think I can handle my housework."

"No, the mother of my child will be waited on like a queen. You are an underboss's wife, anyway. You should have a maid."

"Antonio, you know I hate that word 'underboss.' I prefer that you are called a manager."

"Either way you spell it, you're getting a maid, and that's final."

"You're the boss. But I think I am going to go shopping for some better curtains. I don't care for these."

"That's fine. Do you want one of the boys to take you? I don't want you carrying all kinds of stuff."

"I don't need a guard. I can go shopping all by myself."

"Yeah, I guess. I am just a little nervous now that you're...well, you know."

"Yeah, you can say it, Antonio. The word is 'pregnant.'"

"Yeah that, and I have to get use to this area. It still feels like East Chicago at times. Well, I need to head to the casino and check things out. We are having a big grand opening tomorrow, and I want everything to go well because Mr. Bianchi is coming in. So make sure you have your prettiest dress, because I want you at my side for the celebration."

"Okay, I will wear that nice red one. You better hurry then, and I will see you tonight."

"I will be working late tonight, so if you want to go to bed that will be okay."

"Yeah, I am already kind of tired. I may just do that."

Antonio got up and kissed Maria on the forehead.

"I love you."

"Love you too."

Antonio walked out the door. Maria walked over and picked up the phone to call her mother to give her the news. The phone rang a couple of times before Brigitta picked up.

"Hello. This is Brigitta."

"Hi, Momma. How are you doing?"

"I am doing fine. We miss you terribly around here."

"I miss you all too. I have some news for you. Are you sitting down?"

"Yes, I am…what's going on? Are you all right, Maria?"

"I am pregnant, Momma."

"A grandbaby? You're giving me a grandbaby?"

"Yes, Momma, I just found out yesterday."

"Oh my, now I am really worried. Why don't you leave Antonio and come back here until you have the baby?"

"You know I can't do that. I will be fine. But why don't you plan on coming out here in a couple of months? I will probably need the help even though Antonio is going to get me a maid."

"I will do that. You just let me know when. I need to go and tell everyone. Your sister is going to flip!"

"Okay, Momma. I love you and will talk with you soon."

"I love you too."

Maria hung up the phone and sat there quietly for a moment before she began speaking out loud.

"Okay, as for Antonio…this changes nothing, although having a maid in the house will mess up my work. I would rather my child grows up like me and not with a gangster as a father."

Maria got up and left the room.

***

Hours later, at the Monte Carlo Casino, Antonio and his new caporégime, Michael Chapella, were in his office. Antonio had just been going through the motions for the past few months, but now was ready to take over and make changes.

"Michael, we need to discuss how I want things to operate around here. I know you have been out here all your life and know a lot about the area. So here's the deal…I need you as my right-hand man."

"I appreciate that, Mr. Capresi."

"But I need to have some others. You know, soldiers to take care of the incidentals."

"Well, boss, I have a couple of guys that have been working for me since before the casino business kicked in."

"Tell you what. I want at least four guys, two for each casino. They will be…I guess you could say the head bouncers. Actually, they will be the ones to make sure that we don't get hit by that asshole Caprino, or by that jackass in Reno, Greco. I want them to report directly to you and you to me. Got it?"

"I fully understand. When do you want them to start?"

"They have got to start right away. Don't forget, Mr. Bianchi is coming in tomorrow morning. You will pick him up at the airport with all four guys as protection. I want you all to be dressed to the hilt. There will be nothing but suits around my casinos. We are going to become the classiest operation in town."

"That will not be a problem, boss."

"Okay, now go on down and check the floor. That is where I want you to be most of the time. I have some business to take care of, so I will talk to you later."

"Yes, sir, Mr. Capresi."

Chapella got out of his chair, walked over to the elevator, and entered when the doors opened. Once he was gone, Antonio put his feet on the desk and lit a cigar.

"Now this is the life!"

***

Days had passed, and Maria was a bit homesick, and finally ready to put into motion the plan to put Antonio to rest. She picked up the telephone to call her Gianna. After a few rings Gianna picked up the phone.

"Hello, this is Gianna."

"Hey, Gianna. It's Maria."

"Hey, girl, how are things in Vegas?"

"They are going okay, but there has been a change in things. I'm pregnant."

"Oh my god. Really? What did you go and do that for? What are you going to do?"

"Well, first I am going to become a mommy. Second, I think it's time to kick things into high gear. I need a really big favor from Johnny."

"What do you need? I am sure whatever it is, Johnny or Danny can handle it for you."

"Is it possible for your brother to get close to Mr. Caprino's bunch?"

"Whoa...that's a tall order, girl. But I don't see why not. He has lots of friends from high school, and a couple of them do work for Caprino."

"Okay, this is what I need. I need to find out who the underboss for Caprino is out here in Las Vegas. I am ready to drop the ball on Antonio."

"Are you sure this is the right time?"

"The timing couldn't be better. I want to get this done and come back to Chicago so I can have my baby back there."

"You know it could be very dangerous."

"I know the danger, dear. I have for years. But it is time to stop this game and take care of him. I can't take any more chances since I'm pregnant."

"Okay, I will see what I can do. You know my brother's connections; they will get you what you want. By the way, how's that new house of yours?"

"The house is awesome, and Antonio is going to get me a maid since I told him he was going to be a father. Too bad I am not going to be staying here. Once everything goes down I will probably have to go underground for a bit."

"I can see why. You better be careful, dear, and watch out with the baby."

"I will. Can you get me that info, like right away?"

"I got you covered, my friend. I will call you as soon as I can."

"That's great. Love you, and I will talk to you soon."

Maria hung up the phone.

"Time to let the ball roll, and it is going to roll right over your ass, Antonio."

Chapter Fourteen
Reno and Beyond

In a large office in Reno, Salvatore Greco sat at his desk and talked business with his consigliere, Francesco Vinci.

"Francesco, I hear that there is a new guy in Vegas. It seems that Mr. Bianchi in Chicago has opened a couple of casinos on the strip."

"You heard right, boss. I was talking with some friends down there, and they said that the guy's name is Antonio Capresi. The man's been around for a while, and has quite the name for himself in south Chicago and New York City. It seems he was the one that spearheaded Mr. Bianchi's takeover of the heroin trade."

"Well, that is very interesting. I hope he doesn't get any bright ideas about coming to Reno to take me on. It will be his worst possible day."

***

Later that afternoon Mr. Greco's phone rang.
"Hello."

"I assume this is Mr. Greco?" Antonio said on the other end of the line.

"Yeah, this is Greco, who's this?"

"This is Antonio Capresi. I would like an appointment with you to discuss a business opportunity in Reno."

"So, do you want to meet me at my home?"

"Yes, I think that would be best."

"Okay, I tell you what. You come tomorrow around one o'clock and come clean...no heaters. We can talk about whatever you like."

"That would be fine by me. I shall see you tomorrow. You have a blessed day, Mr. Greco."

"Yeah, whatever." Salvatore hung up the phone, then yelled for his consigliere.

"Francesco, get in here!"

Within seconds Francesco came into his office.

"Yeah, boss, what is up?"

"It seems that our friend from Chicago, Mr. Capresi, wants a meeting with me. He will be here tomorrow at one o'clock. I will want you and the boys to be here to check him out. No monkey business."

"You got it, boss. We will be ready for him if he tries anything stupid."

"Good. Now do me a favor and get me a Scotch neat."

"Whatever you need, Mr. Greco."

Francesco poured the drink for his boss, then set it on his desk.

"Grazie." Greco took the glass.

"You're welcome. Is there anything else?"

"No, you can leave."

Francesco turned and left the office.

"If that Antonio tries anything, I will have him wearing cement overshoes at the bottom of Lake Tahoe," Greco said with a grin.

***

As Greco was grinning over his drink, Nicholas Valachio and Jerry Fezzulgio were sitting in Giovanni Caprino's office.

"Okay, fellas. I hear that our friend Bianchi has added operations in Vegas, and is trying to hone in on Reno too. We need to do something about that. Jerry, I need you to go to Vegas and meet with Glen Decencio. I want info on what is going on and who is running their operation out there."

Jerry stood up right away. "I will leave right away, boss."

"Good. Nicholas, while he is gone I want you to go see what you can find out around here. I want to know what the scat is out on the street."

"You got it, boss."

"Grazie...I want to know right away."

Nicholas and Jerry kissed Caprino's ring and left the room.

Giovanni then took a sip of wine. "I'll get that son of a bitch Bianchi one of these days!"

***

Gianna and her brother, Johnny, were in her kitchen having a cup of coffee.

"So, Johnny, I get this call from Maria this morning. She says that it is time for her to take out Antonio."

"Is she sure? I mean, this could be dangerous, maybe even deadly."

"She says she knows what she is doing. But she needs your help."

"Sure, whatever she needs."

"I am glad you said that. Can you get with your friends David or Tony Buscetti?"

"You know I hate those two, but David and I were best friends in high school. What does she want to know?"

"She needs the name of Caprino's underboss out in Vegas. I think she is going to flip Antonio."

"Wow. That is a big order, sis. I don't know if they will tell me."

"Tell them you are planning a trip out there and want only the best."

"That's as good as anything I could come up with. I will see what I can do."

***

Later that evening at the Eldorado Club, Johnny was sitting at the bar alone when Tony Buscetti walked in. Johnny waved for him to join him, and Tony walked over and sat down beside him.

"Well, if it isn't the speedster Johnny Racan."

"Hey, Tony! Let me buy you a drink. What's your poison?"

"Thanks, Johnny. I just need bourbon on the rocks."

Johnny waved the bartender over.

"I need two bourbons on the rocks for my friend and me."

The bartender pulled out another glass. He filled Johnny's first, then put some ice in the other and poured one for Tony.

"There you go."

Tony took his glass. "Thanks, man."

Johnny turned to face Tony.

"It's been a while. How are things going for you?"

"Yeah, it has been a long time. Things are going well. I've been quite busy. How about you? You working hard or hardly working?"

"Well, I have been so busy I'm thinking it is time to take me a vacation."

"Is that a fact? Where are you thinking of heading?"

"I am actually thinking of going to Las Vegas to do some gambling."

"Is that right? You know, I have some friends in Vegas that could show you around."

"Yeah, Tony, but I just want it to be top notch. There are so many real dives out there from what I have heard."

"I tell you what. I will make a call to my buddy, Glen Decencio. He is a good friend of mine, and he's the manager over at the Flamingo. He'll treat you right."

"That sounds great. I will head out that way next Monday."

"Cool. I will call him tomorrow and set things up. When you get to the Flamingo, tell them you want to speak with Glen and that Mr. Caprino sent you."

"I will. Thanks. A toast to the old high school days."

"To old days."

The two raised their glasses and drank.

***

Later that night, Antonio and Maria were at the dining room table.

"Babe, I need to take a little trip. Just for two days."

"Where are you going now?"

"I am going up to Reno to check out land for a couple of casinos."

"Are you leaving tomorrow?"

"Yeah, but like I said, it is just for two days."

"Okay, I will get your bag together tonight."

"Thanks, babe. You are way too good for me."

"Oh, I know that…just kidding."

"Yeah, you're a funny gal."

***

The following afternoon there was a knock at the door of Salvatore Greco's home. Joseph Romano and Michael Mancini, his two soldiers, sat with Greco at his desk.

"Yeah, come in," Greco yelled out.

Mr. Greco's capo, Mario Rossi, opened the door and stepped into the office.

"Boss, there is a gentleman at the door by the name of Antonio Capresi. He said that you are expecting him. Should I let him in?"

"Yeah, but I want you to take these two and pat that bastard down good. I want all you three in the room with me the whole time. I don't want any monkey business out of this guy. In fact, find Francesco and have him in here too."

"You got it. Come on, guys."

The three men left the room and went out to the foyer, where Francesco joined them. They all approached Antonio.

Mario was the first to speak. "The boss says he will see you. But first, we need to make sure you aren't carrying any heat."

"I'm clean, but if you must."

"That's what the man said. Now get against the wall and spread 'em," Joseph said.

"What? You guys think you're cops or something?"

"No, but we can be your worst nightmare," Michael piped in.

Francesco then stepped in. "Just do as they say. They haven't had lunch yet and get quite cranky."

Antonio walked to the wall, placed his hands on it, and spread his legs while Mancini started to pat him down. "Whatever."

"He's clean, boss."

"I told you I was. Now tell your thugs to back off."

"Antonio, you need to watch your mouth or you're not going anywhere."

"Just take me to your boss."

The five men left the foyer and entered Mr. Greco's office. Greco stood as Antonio got to his desk. Mancini and Romano sat on each side of his desk as Rossi parked himself by the door. Francesco took a seat beside Antonio's chair.

"So, you are the notorious Antonio Capresi. I have heard that you got quite the name for yourself back in Chi-town."

"I did what needed to be done, and I didn't take any crap."

Mr. Greco sat down.

"That is good...I respect that from a man. Please have a seat."

Antonio moved to a large leather chair in front of the desk and sat.

Mr. Greco continued. "So what, may I ask, is the reason you requested this little meeting with me?"

"I'm not here to cause any trouble, and I don't want to step on any toes. I come here representing Mr. Bianchi. We want to work with you on allowing us to build a couple of casinos in this region."

"So you want to take away some of my business?"

"I wouldn't put it that way, Mr. Greco. Let's just call it a mutual agreement. We are even willing to promote your clubs from Vegas and give you a five percent cut...let's call it a bonus."

"You're going to give us promotion and five percent, while you could be taking ten times that from my casinos? What have you been drinking?"

The other men all started to laugh.

"I think it would be mutually beneficial to work together, instead of us coming in and taking the whole thing," Antonio replied.

Mr. Greco stood up behind his desk, and both Mancini and Romano stepped to the front of the desk. "Listen here, you little son of a bitch. You tell your boss if you try to hit us, it would be your biggest mistake."

"Mr. Greco, please...that is not what we want. I tell you what. I am willing to raise the offer to ten percent in exchange for just a little southern territory to build two casinos, and that's it."

"You would give us ten percent of all Reno take, and promotion for our casinos from yours in Vegas?"

"Yes, sir, that is my final offer."

"You know something, Antonio? You have really got some guts coming to my home, kid. I like it. I tell you what...you go call your boss and tell him we have a deal. I will have Mr. Vinci, my consigliere here, line out the details."

"I am glad we could work things out. If any of your guys or yourself are ever down in Vegas, please come to the Monte Carlo. I will comp you for whatever you need."

"I assure you, Mr. Capresi, I will be keeping an eye on you. Now if you don't mind...Rossi, see this man to his car."

"Grazie, Mr. Greco," Antonio said.

Antonio and Rossi both got up and walked out of the office.

Mr. Greco turned to his other guys. "Romano, Mancini; I want to take him up on his offer. The two of you make a visit to Vegas next week and check this guy out."

"Yes, sir, Mr. Greco."

"You guys take off. I have some business to take care of with Francesco."

"Yes, sir."

The two men walked out of the room and closed the door behind them.

"Francesco, draw up a contract stating they can't hit us or back out of the deal. I want it iron clad. Got it?"

"No problem, Mr. Greco."

Francesco got up from his seat and left the office.

***

An hour later, Antonio was in his hotel room. He picked up the phone to report to Mr. Bianchi.

"Pasquale Bianchi, what do you need?"

"Mr. Bianchi, this is Antonio."

"Yes, Antonio, how are things in Nevada?"

"Everything is working out great, sir. I just finished meeting with Mr. Greco, and have secured a small area of land for your two new casinos in Reno. He accepted your offer of ten percent of Reno's take, and advertisement from Las Vegas for his places."

"You are doing a very good job, Antonio. You have impressed me over and over again. Now I want you to work with the people out there to develop the two casinos. I want one to be called the "Eldorado Club," just like our little hole in the wall here. The

172

second casino name I will leave up to your imagination."

"How does 'The Bonanza' sound to you?"

"That will work for me. Now get to work and get my casinos up and running as soon as possible."

"I will get things going right away, Mr. Bianchi. We should be in the casinos there within a year, maybe sooner."

"That is good. I will talk to you later when you get back to Las Vegas."

"Yes, sir, I will call you in a week with the monthly report. Goodbye."

"Ciao."

Antonio hung up the phone and began to pack for his trip home.

***

The following day, Maria had decided that it was time to put an end to the charade. She called her sister Theresa. "Hello."

"Hey, sis. How are you?"

"I am doing fine."

"Okay, so, sis; Gianna is going to get me the name of Mr. Bianchi's competition out here in Las Vegas, and I am rolling Antonio."

"Are you sure? That is going to be dangerous."

"Well, my plan is that I am going to contact the Caprino Vegas underboss, and let him know that it was Antonio that shot Caprino's son and where he can be found. Then I am going to pick a fight with Antonio and fly home to wait for them to hit him."

"That sure sounds like a good plan, as long as your timing is right."

"Just remember, if by some chance anything happens to me, get that package I gave you to Judge James Mullins. He will finish off the rest of the Bianchi family."

"Nothing had better happen to you, and you can bring this to the judge yourself when you get your little ass back here. You know Mom really misses you."

"Yeah, I know. Just tell her I love her and that I will be home real soon."

"Okay, I will. Well, I have to head out and do some shopping. You just need to be careful, sis. Love ya!"

"Have fun and I will talk to you soon. Love ya back! Ciao."

Maria hung up the phone. Just a few moments later the phone rang at Maria's, and she picked it up.

"Hello."

"Hey, Maria, it's Johnny. Can you talk?"

"Hey, Johnny. Yeah, I can talk. Antonio is in Reno today doing his monkey business. You find out anything for me?"

"Yeah, I got him. You will need to go to the Flamingo and ask for Glen Decencio. He is Caprino's man out there. But I warn you, they don't play nice. I was lucky to find this out from one of Caprino's men who I was best friends with in high school."

"Johnny, come on, you know I have been around these guys all my life. I know what I am doing."

"Yeah, I know you're a smart cookie. Just be careful for me and Gianna, okay?"

"You got it. I appreciate the information, and I should be back in Chicago before you know it."

"Great. I gotta run. Talk to you soon."

"You got it. Good-bye."

"Catch ya later, alligator," Johnny said as he hung up the phone.

Maria hung the phone up.

"Now I got you, Antonio. Your days are numbered, and I am going to make you pay dearly."

G. R. Holton & Marlene Mendoza

Chapter Fifteen
The End of the Game

Later that afternoon, Maria walked up to the service desk of the Flamingo Casino and got the attention of the concierge who was standing at the front desk.

"Young man, I need to speak to Glen Decencio."

"Excuse me, madam?"

"I said I need to see Mr. Decencio. What part of that didn't you understand?"

"I am sorry, but no one sees Mr. Decencio without an appointment."

"He will see me. Tell him I have info from Mr. Bianchi."

"One second, ma'am."

The concierge picked up the phone and called Decencio's office. Within a couple of rings Decencio picked up the phone.

"What do you need?"

"Yes, Mr. Decencio, I hate to bother you, but there is a young woman here that says she needs to speak with you about some guy named Mr. Bianchi."

"What's her name?"

The concierge turned to Maria.

"What is your name?"

"Tell him that is not important at this time. I have some very important info he wants about Stephano Caprino."

"One moment."

The concierge put the phone back to his ear.

"Sir, she will not give her name, but says she has information on a Stephano Caprino."

"Is that so? Okay, have her wait right there. I will send someone for her."

"Yes, sir."

The concierge hung up the phone.

"Someone will be here shortly."

"Thank you."

***

Moments later, David Buscetti walked up to Maria.

"Mr. Buscetti, this is the young woman I told Mr. Decencio about."

"Follow me, ma'am."

"Lead the way, tall, dark, and gruesome," Maria said, laughing.

"Oh, so you're a funny gal."

"I try my best. Now take me to Mr. Decencio."

Maria followed Buscetti to the elevator and he took her to the penthouse level where they stepped out into Mr. Decencio's office. Glen Decencio was on his couch with a young blonde, and he waved for Maria to come over.

"Okay, babe, you need to go powder your nose downstairs. This young woman and I have some business to discuss."

The young blonde got up off the couch, fixed her dress, and went into the elevator.

"Have a seat. I am Glen Decencio, manager of the Flamingo. Would you like a drink?"

"No thanks. This is not a social call. I have info for you and your boss, Mr. Caprino."

"That's what I heard. What do you know about Stephano?"

"I know exactly who killed him, and can tell you where to find him."

"Is that right? Do tell, because I am all ears."

"Not so fast, Mr. Decencio. Like I said, this is business. I expect to be paid for this information."

"Okay. How much do you want, dollface?"

"I need you to give me twenty-five thousand."

"Well now, that is kind of pricey. How do I know you're not just some sick bitch trying to get rid of a boyfriend?"

"Listen. Stephano was shot in Chicago coming out of the Normandy House Restaurant. How would someone from Las Vegas know about that?"

"Okay, point well made. So tell me what you have and I will see to it that you get paid."

"No, it doesn't work that way. You are going to give me the money, and then I will give you the information."

"You're a shrewd businesswoman. Okay, we can do this. David, go downstairs and get twenty-five thousand. Put my name on it. Mr. Caprino would gladly let me pay to hear this one."

"Okay, boss. Be right back."

David Buscetti turned and got back into the elevator.

"While we are waiting, I have very good champagne that is already chilled. Call it a toast to a business transaction."

"I can't. I am pregnant and can't drink."

"I hope you don't mind if I do?"

"Be my guest. It's your casino."

Glen got up, walked over to his bar, and poured himself a glass of champagne. He walked back to the couch and sat down.

"I still haven't gotten your name."

"The name is Maria. The last name is of no consequence."

"Well, Maria, a toast to business."

Glen took a sip of champagne as the elevator opened and David Buscetti walked back into the room with a stack of bills.

"Here you go, boss; twenty-five thousand, just like you said."

David handed the bills to Decencio.

"Thanks, David. Now go ahead downstairs and check the floor. I can handle this."

"Okay, boss."

David turned around and left through the elevator doors. Glen then handed the bills to Maria.

"Okay, now, here is your money. I want all the details."

Maria placed the bills into her purse.

"The hit was put out by Mr. Bianchi."

"Come on now, Maria, we figured that. If that is all you have, then give me back my damn money."

"No, that is not all I have, Mr. Decencio. I know who the shooter was."

"Enough of the games, Maria. Just spill the beans."

"The shooter was Antonio Capresi. He shot him in the alleyway just down from the restaurant. But he is no longer in Chicago. He is now the underboss for Mr. Bianchi here in Las Vegas."

"You don't say. Where can I find him?"

"I can set it up, but he can be found at the Monte Carlo Club. He is managing that casino for Bianchi."

"Okay, you call me and set up a time when Capresi can be found at his office, and my boys will take care of the rest."

"I will get it set up for you."

Maria got up from the couch. "Thank you for the money. It is a pleasure doing business with you."

"Come back any time. But if you don't call me in a day or so, I assure you that I will come find you."

"Don't you worry; I have been waiting for this day for a long time."

Glen got up from the couch and walked Maria to the elevator.

"Have a good day, Maria."

"I plan on it."

***

181

As Maria walked into the elevator, Decencio walked over to his desk and picked up the phone to call Mr. Caprino. "Mr. Caprino, this is Glen in Vegas. I hate to bother you, but I have some information you will want to hear."

"What do you have, Glen?"

"I just met with a young woman by the name of Maria. She told me that a gentleman by the name of Antonio Capresi was the shooter of your son, Stephano."

"Antonio Capresi...that son of a bitch is one of Bianchi's boys. Where is he right now?"

"Well, luckily, he is out here in Las Vegas running the Monte Carlo."

"Is that so? Well, that is good for us. I want him hit right away."

"The young woman said she will call me when he is in his office."

"Don't wait that long. I want him hit tomorrow night. Get the boys together and hit him hard."

"As you wish, boss! Oh, by the way, I had to put out twenty-five thousand to get this information. I hope you don't mind."

"That is fine. You need to contact me when the job is done. Good-bye."

Decencio hung up the phone and then called down to the concierge.

"Tell David Buscetti to come up to my office right away."

"I will take care of that, Mr. Decencio."

Within moments David Buscetti walked out of the elevator.

"You wanted to see me, boss?"

"That young lady has brought me some interesting info, and Mr. Caprino wants to tie up some loose ends."

"What do we need to do?"

"It seems that the man who shot Mr. Caprino's son Stephano is now an underboss out here. So, I need you to get a couple of the boys together. We are going to hit the Monte Carlo tomorrow night, and we are going to hit it hard."

"As you wish, boss. I will go round them up."

David turned and left the office.

"Mr. Capresi, tonight is your last night. I hope you enjoy it," Decencio said as he took another sip of champagne.

***

About an hour later Maria walked into the First National Bank of Nevada. Once inside she walked up to one of the tellers, a young blonde lady, and handed her the whole $25,000.

"I need to get a cashier's check please, for twenty-five thousand."

"Are you sure you wouldn't like to deposit some of that? We provide a great interest rate for savings accounts."

"No thanks. I just hit it big at the Flamingo and I'm sending it to my mother. But thanks for asking."

The teller made out the cashier's check and handed it to Maria.

"Well, if you ever hit it big again, just remember us."

"I will. Thanks so much."

"Have a great day."

Maria turned away and placed the check into an envelope addressed to her mother. Stepping back out into the Nevada heat, she kissed the envelope and placed it into the mailbox right in front of the bank.

***

Later that night Michael Chapella walked into Antonio's office. Antonio was seated at his desk.

"Hey, boss. Do you have a minute?"

"Sure, Michael, what's going on?"

"Well, I just got through talking to one of the boys, and he told me that he saw a woman that looked just like Maria going into the Flamingo today."

"My Maria, at the Flamingo?"

"That's what he said. He stood there for a while and she came walking out a half hour later."

"Does he know where she went from there?"

"Yeah, he followed her from a distance right down the street to the bank."

"Is that right?"

"Yes, and then she came out and put an envelope into the mailbox."

"I guess I need to get her down here and find out what the hell she was doing there. Why don't you go check the floor? I have a call to make."

"No problem, boss."

Michael proceeded out of the office. Antonio picked up his phone and called Maria. After a few rings Maria picked up.

"Hello, this is Maria."

"Hey, babe. What you up to?"

"Just got back from town."

"I was thinking...why don't you come to the Monte Carlo and we can have some dinner? It has been a while since we went out."

"Sure thing. I will be down there in a little while."

"Okay, doll. See you then."

Antonio hung up his phone.

"She better not have been up to no good, because I swear if she was, I will kill her myself."

***

Later that evening Maria and Antonio were at the table in the Monte Carlo's restaurant.

"So, what did you do today?" Antonio asked.

"Oh, I went walking around window shopping, and checked out a couple of the other casinos."

"Like the Flamingo?"

"Yeah...wait a minute, are you having me followed?"

"No. It's just that one of my boys saw you go into the Flamingo and come back out soon afterwards."

"Well, if that doesn't beat all. Yeah, I went in there and I had some money and decided to play a little roulette. I hit a couple of numbers, and then went to the bank to send my momma a little something. Is that okay?"

"Actually, Maria, it isn't. That casino is owned by Mr. Caprino."

"So what does that have to do with me? I think it is pretty, all pink and stuff."

"Listen to me. You stay out of the other casinos. It doesn't look good for business. On top of that, you are giving money to the competition. If you ever want to play roulette, you bring yourself down here. Capiche?"

"I just didn't think anything of it. The last thing I want to do is cause you problems, dear. But I did win money, so that actually took money from Mr. Caprino."

"Yeah, you did. You are way too smart. Okay, enough said. Let's finish eating and go catch a show."

"That sounds good to me."

Antonio and Maria went back to their meal.

***

The following morning Decencio and Buscetti were in the office discussing the hit on Antonio.

"This is how I want it to go down tonight. You take a couple of boys and plug the bouncers out front first. Once they are down, I want you to go in and off the concierge. Then, go up the elevator and finish off Capresi. Any questions?"

"Yeah, I have one. What if he's not alone?"

"Too bad for whoever is there. I want one hit, and make it hard. You need to make sure that son of a bitch is dead. Comprende?"

"We can do that, boss. I will have everything ready at eight. That way it is dark enough so no one sees our faces. It will be a quick hit. Over and done with."

"That's just the way I want it. Once you are done, be on the down low for a couple of days. Maybe take a little trip, say to California or something. I don't want you coming back here too quickly."

"Understood."

"Mr. Caprino will finally have vengeance for Stephano's death."

***

It was evening in Las Vegas, and Maria walked out of the elevator and into Antonio's office.

"Hey there, babe, what are you doing down here?"

"I was bored sitting around the house watching the maid, and figured I may gamble a little bit. Can I have some chips?"

Antonio laughed. "At least you are coming to the right place this time. But I can see what you mean about boredom, sitting in that big house all the time. Hold on a second."

Antonio went over to a picture on the wall and pulled it to him, which revealed a safe in the wall. He opened the safe and took out a thousand dollars in chips.

"Okay, babe. Here you go. Just try not to lose it all at once, okay?"

"I'll try not to."

***

Outside the casino, two guards stood at the doorway, when suddenly a long black vehicle pulled up with machine guns stuck out the window. They opened fire on the two men, killing them instantly. The car stopped for three guys to get out and enter the casino.

Once inside they approached the concierge, brandishing a pistol.

"Hey, what the hell are you guys doing?" yelled the concierge.

Before he could say anything else, they shot him with a pistol equipped with a silencer, so as not to attract more attention than they already had outside. Once he fell to the floor, they pulled him behind the counter, and then shot the attendant behind the counter. The three men then boarded the elevator.

Within seconds, just as Maria turned around to leave, the men came out of the elevator and fired on Maria and Antonio, who was standing behind her. The bullets hit Maria in the chest and stomach, while Antonio was shot in the shoulders, and the two of them fell to the floor. Antonio was under Maria, who quickly lost a lot of blood that spilled over both of them. Stepping toward the couple on the floor to finish the job, the gunmen backtracked and beat a hasty retreat down the stairs as the elevator sounded. Once the men were gone, Antonio got to his knees and lifted Maria up to his chest.

"Oh my god! I am so sorry, Maria."

"It was supposed to be you, you son of a bitch. You shot my father when I was ten years old, and I have waited all my life to pay you back."

Maria stopped breathing, and Antonio closed her eyes with his hand, crying.

"That had to be Caprino's guys. I will get them for killing my wife and child!"

***

A few hours later Mr. Caprino was behind his desk with the phone at his ear, with Glen Decencio on the other end.

"So Glen, tell me what happened. I want the whole story."

"Well, our boys took out the guards at the front door, and then took out the concierge and the attendant behind the counter so they couldn't call up to Antonio."

"Okay, that sounds good so far...continue."

"They got into the elevator, and when the doors opened up they sprayed the room. They killed a woman that was there—I think it was his wife—and then had to make a break for it down the stairwell because the elevator was opening and they couldn't stick around."

"So, let me get this straight. Your guys went in and shot up the place, killing Capresi's girl, but you're not sure if you got Capresi himself?"

"That's right, boss. Before they could check him, his boys or the cops came up the elevator, and they had to escape down the stairwell."

"I understand. I think that is a good thing for the moment. If Capresi is still alive, then I want to let him suffer the way I have. You did well; make sure all your guys have iron-clad alibis."

"Thanks, boss. If you want us to hit him again we can."

"No, just wait until I call you. We have to use caution, because I'm sure the cops are all over this by now. Just go ahead and get back to work, and we will talk soon."

"Will do, boss."

Caprino pressed the button to close the call, and then called his consigliere, Eddy Marshone. Within seconds Marshone was on the phone.

"Hello, Marshone residence."

"Eddy, I need you to come to my office. We have some business to discuss."

"Boss, it is three in the morning. Can we talk when I get in?"

"No, Eddy, I am sorry but I need you in here right now. We have issues in Las Vegas."

"Okay, boss. I can be there in an hour."

"See you then."

Mr. Caprino hung up the phone.

"I am going to put a little surprise visit together for Bianchi that he won't soon forget."

***

A few days later there were many people, including Maria's mother, Antonio, and some of Mr. Bianchi's men, at the funeral ceremony. The casket was open, showing the beautiful Maria and her slightly protruding stomach. Brigitta was in her seat, crying profusely.

The priest performed the ceremony as everyone looked on.

"We are all at a loss for words from losing such a loving soul, and a child that never got a chance to see this world. May they rest in peace, and their souls find rest with our Lord. Amen.

"I want to thank everyone for coming. There will be a gathering at the home of Brigitta Cachiotti. This ends the service."

Theresa helped her mother to her feet, but Brigitta fell to her knees at her daughter's casket, weeping.

Hours later, everyone gathered at Brigitta's apartment for a traditional funeral gathering. About twenty people were milling about the living room. Brigitta walked around and thanked those who came, until she came to Antonio. She froze in front of him, and then slapped him across his face, a look of hatred on her face.

"You're the son of a bitch that should have been in that casket. It is your entire fault that my husband, my little girl, and my grandbaby are dead. I told her to leave you, but she wouldn't listen. I told her not to go to Las Vegas with you. I knew this would happen."

Theresa walked over and took her mother by the arm to lead her away. "Come on, Momma. You don't need to be talking to this piece of trash. In fact, Antonio, you need to leave right now. We don't ever want to see your face again!"

Theresa and Brigitta walked away.

***

The next morning Theresa walked into the office of Judge James Mullins and went to the secretary's desk.

"I have a package here for Judge Mullins."

"Okay. Who can I say it's from?"

"Just tell him it contains information about mob bosses Caprino and Bianchi."

"I will make sure he gets it. Do you want to wait?"

"No, but thank you."

Theresa left the office and the secretary took the package into the judge's chambers. She walked in and placed the large manila envelope on the judge's desk.

"A woman just delivered this for you, and said it had to do with Caprino and Bianchi."

The judge opened the envelope and dumped all the photos and the notebook out onto his desk. He looked at some photos, then opened the notebook and read some of the entries. He tossed the book on his desk and smiled.

"Well, I will be a monkey's uncle. Get me the chief of police on the phone."

"Right away, sir."

"Those boys are going to fry this time."

THE END

ABOUT THE AUTHORS

Bob(G. R.)Holton

On a warm summer morning in 1962, I was born in a small town in Massachusetts, and I am the second eldest in a family of eight children. I am a happily married husband and I live in East Tennessee with my wife, mother, and my Shih-poo named "Ewok". I have two daughters, a son, a step-daughter and a step-son, and am also the proud grandfather of three beautiful girls.

I am a disabled veteran who has taken an interest in computer games to pass the time. One day I made a friend on one of those online games with chat that turned out to be screenwriter and movie director Derek Milton. He and I became great friends, and after a few weeks of talking he gave me a couple of his screenplays to read, and I was hooked. I knew at that point I wanted to try writing.

After days of not being able to come up with a story to write, I had a dream of three teens on another planet and in a cave. That was it; I knew what had to be done. I sat down at the computer, and over the course of three months I wrote my first book, Soleri. I knew I couldn't stop there, so I continued writing and

Guardians Alliance was born. I have also published a children's picture book called, Squazles, about not judging others, and did the book design for Cameron Titus's A to Z book: A Habitat for Humanity Project. My fourth novel, Deep Screams, is a science fiction/horror/paranormal thriller that became the Books and Authors.net's Best Science Fiction release for 2011. I was also voted by The Author's Show's "50 Best Writers You Should be Reading for 2011". My fifth release is called, Dragon's Bow a tale of sister vs. sister and good vs. evil. My latest is a collaboration novel and screenplay with Producer Marlene Mendoza called, The Mob, a 1930s tale of a woman's revenge for the death of her father.

In my other life, I have taken on writing screenplays which have been done for three of my books, Deep Screams, Dragon's Bow, and Teleported (based on Soleri); all have been optioned for movies by Gilt entertainment. I have also written an additional screenplay optioned based on the novel, The Galaxy Watch: A Galacteran Legacy that is owned by Gilt Entertainment.

All of my works can be found at all the Internet book sale sites or on my website at www.grholton.com.

MARLENE MENDOZA

On a cool Fall morning in 1952, Marlene was born in the city of Montreal and she is the third to the youngest of seven children. She grew up in the suburbs of Chateauguay, Quebec, Canada and loved the outdoors. She joined the local girl's hockey team, played baseball in the summer and learned ballet, piano, and sang in the choir. She learned to love music and read books from an early age reading 2-3 books a week thinking someday she would love to get involved in her own novel.

Her mother, Margaret Pacholka, was a school teacher for many years and she taught 4 grades in one class in French and English. She dedicates my accomplishments to her, because she always taught her to read from an early age. Her father worked in aerospace for most of his life, and in 1965 they moved to California. She followed his footsteps and worked in aerospace for almost ten years. She dedicates her enthusiasm to live life to its fullest from her dad. She then went into the finance industry and studied business and law at La Verne University.

Marlene Mendoza holds a MSM, BSM, CSA, SHRM and CRMC. She is a film producer, Executive Producer with Gilt Entertainment. She has a Master's of Science in Management (Leadership), (Summa cum

Laude 4.0) and a Bachelor's of Science in Management (Sales and Marketing). She is a Certified Risk Management Specialist.

Her company Gilt Entertainment is an independent global film development, high-end story and production company. They have a strong diversified presence in motion picture production, and digital distribution for home and family entertainment. They provide production, business consulting, transformation leadership skills, sales and marketing management, marketing director, and talent management services. They have a blueprint for growth that combines the flexibility and entrepreneurial culture of an independent company with financial and strategic relationships worldwide.

Gilt Entertainment's mission statement is to put ethics first and foremost within our global teams, in marketing research, preparation, writing, interviewing, presenting, development and production of the product or service.

Our promise is to create stories with substance, and give creative freedom to actors and filmmakers along with a share in our profits.

Marlene Mendoza is producing the upcoming film titled "The Mob" now in Pre-production which is based off an adaptation the novel authored by Marlene Mendoza and G. R. Holton. She is producing "The Mob" based on 1930's era with co-producer Director Larry McLean, Gary Van Haas, Tony Severio and Randall Oliver scheduled for release late 2014. As well as developing the screen adaptation of a book "Galaxy Watch (The Galacteran Legacy). She acquired financing for "Galaxy Watch" scheduled for release 2015 after "The Mob".

In addition, Marlene is working with Gary on "Malabar Run" a psychological thriller. Plus working on "The Maul" which is a Socio-political ethnic drama and "Showdown in Durango" for Mexico. Plus, a crime thriller drama film called "The Club" for Las Vegas.

Marlene's newest venture is working on the film "The Family" with Thomas Raft Producer/Actor of Jefatov Films and Niels U. Basse of Azazello Productions. It's a Socio-drama film set for Scandinavian country with A-list cast and director.

Plus she is producing "Fearless Heart" in development that is a Socio-drama film about 1929 and the Great Depression. The moral of the story is to have faith. Marlene Mendoza also has a fantasy film and two sci-fi films open for co-production.

There are new major films on the horizon with major director/cast in place, including a digital distribution company. Marlene has recently j/v with AIM Digitech out of India to produce a film called DevilShare that will be made into a Television series. The video has been shown on India television and is now hitting the film festivals for a TV deal.

As of this writing Marlene is in talks for a reality TV show and it will benefit an environmental organization with a veteran component. She will be the Producer of the show.

Besides running her own independent film development company, Gilt Entertainment, she also heads her own worldwide talent management firm. She has two lovely children Dan and Michelle who have made her proud and she lives in Palm Springs, CA.

http://giltentertainmentcorp.com

CPSIA information can be obtained at www.ICGtesting.com
Printed in the USA
LVOW08s1950140916

504612LV00004B/135/P